THE MEN WHO TAKE EYES

JUSTIN LITTLE

CLASH

Copyright © 2020 by Justin Little

ISBN: 978-1-944866-77-8

Cover: Mathew Revert

matthewrevertdesign.com

CLASH Books

clashbooks.com

Troy, NY

"A man, after he has brushed off the dust and chips of his life, will have left only the hard, clean questions: Was it good or was it evil? Have I done well or ill?"

JOHN STEINBECK

PART ONE

CHAPTER ONE

Two men died as Oliver changed the channel on the television set. The old television was hanging directly above the bookshelves that housed the History section of the library. A couple of scouts sent by the Vigil to report back on the perimeter defenses were picked off by patrolling sentries. Sometimes there would be music playing through the television and radio, but this morning the television greeted him with a symphony of static. He turned the shrieking box off and straightened his thin-framed glasses.

The monotony of library work was a curse in itself, especially when no one had checked anything out for over twenty years. A strong scent of mildew constantly invaded Oliver's nose. Dust caked nearly every single book in the small and poorly lit room. A spectrum of color from dull yellow to dark tan covered the fraying, folded, and ripped pages. Although the words inside of these tomes were very much alive, the carpet of dust spread over them made the books themselves appear dead. No one was interested in reviving these corpses during times of strife. The information was considered useless because it was. When a large group of modern men wants you dead how useful is skimming through a treatise on what the best economic structure for an agrarian society is? Not even Oliver could muster up the courage to perform such a useless action even when surrounded by the worst kind of boredom. In a way, the world was dusty. Dusty and rigid. All softness had been ground out of it and even the skin of the average person appeared hardened, in the same way a patch of mud after an evening rain splinters in the next afternoon's sun. Nothing bent. Everything either stood firm or snapped in two. There was a war on, and war makes everything terrifying and dull.

A line was forming outside of the library awaiting this week's shipment of pamphlets. Everyone had seen the car delivering said pamphlets turn down the alley between the library and the adjacent apartment building. Frustration bubbled among those waiting in line. Oliver arose from his desk and strolled towards the thick metal door which led to the alleyway. As he opened the door, the car was already speeding away. The pamphlets were wrapped in two large plastic bags which were thrown carelessly on the gravel road. A note was taped to the top of one of the bags that read, "Deliver to O. Walters."

Oliver grabbed both bags, shuffled back into the library, and slammed the door behind him with his foot. Not being a very strong man, that door was the most difficult part of his work day. His scrawny arms shook slightly when lifting the heavy load of paper. He hurled the bags onto the table in the middle of the room and ripped open the packaging. It was a pleasure to see fresh white paper again. It was like seeing a young optimistic schoolchild after wading through a pile of rotting bodies. Pamphlets and books had different natures anyhow, and people preferred the thing more easily forgotten, crumpled up, and discarded. Each pamphlet had the words "Insurrection Weekly Report" written in red across the front. Oliver knew since the delivery was late he would be late in opening the library again. It was the third time this month.

After taking the time to stack the pamphlets neatly, and shoving one into his back pocket, Oliver opened up the library. People began pouring in, making sure to let Oliver know what they thought of him as they walked by. Some of them mumbled insults. One man went so far as to call out for his removal as librarian. They were already grabbing pamphlets from the table and reading them with enthusiasm. Encased in every pamphlet were a few photographs, a general report about the status of the revolution, and an opinion piece written by de facto leader Nicholas Stevens. Both Oliver and Nicholas had a personal boiling hatred for the Vigil.

Oliver was present when Nicholas publicly stood in defiance of tyranny by carving off the mandatory tattoo for all citizens from the back of his hand. He was a child then and Nicholas had to have been in his late twenties. As soon as Oliver could grab a knife and sneak away from his parents, he did the same as everyone who defected and joined the Insurrection. The imperfect circular pink scar present on his right hand was a constant reminder of that emotion. Even a permanent disfigurement was more desirable than the ominous jagged *V* forced upon everyone at birth when the Vigil had taken over free society. The left arm of the letter was thick, the right one was thin, and it was always colored black. Merely seeing the letter in Nicholas' last name made him wince in reflexive anger. Slumping in his desk chair Oliver began to read the report:

"Minor skirmishes on the front line on Wednesday of last week. Insurrection Death Toll: 32. Enemy Death Toll: 57. Defectors: 0. New Members of the Insurrection: 124. Meat supply running low. New Members are asked to bring food if at all possible during their escape. Our men continue to disrupt checkpoints to make escape safer. The Vigil continues attempts at sabotaging our supply lines. Large explosion heard within Vigil territory, investigation pending. Possible weapons testing. Rumors of Vigil espionage. Morale remains high among..."

"Did you see it?" a nasally voice exclaimed knocking Oliver out of his reading session, "What did you think?"

"Did I see what, Edward? I was in the middle of something," Oliver replied

"The picture!" Edward fumbled in his pants for his copy of the pamphlet. "Right here, the photograph of Circle Park. I took this one, and it got featured in the weekly report! I've been waiting for this for years now, can you believe it? Finally the Insurrection can make use of me. Tell me what you think."

"I'm sure it feels fantastic," Oliver remarked as he glanced down at the black and white photograph. A mostly dead tree dotted with stray patches of leaves stood in the center of a ring of well-trimmed grass. Supporters of the revolution sat together talking, and a few children were playing with various toys. Circle Park was where the uprising against the Vigil first began. Ten courageous people were shot dead on that grass. Their gravestones formed a semi-circle around the tree.

Oliver remembers sitting at a school desk when it

happened: the primordial movement buried them there as a symbol of hope, their bodies providing fertilizer for one of the only live trees left. Hatred gurgled in his chest for both himself and the Vigil. He considered his cowardice to be an act of complicity in this atrocity by remaining a bystander despite only being a child at the time. Although, when trying to recount what the protesters were shot for he couldn't remember. It has been widely accepted that they were standing their ground in opposition to their publication being shut down, but everyone had a slightly different story about them. Some thought they were trying to get someone out of jail, others that they were taunting Vigil agents in order to provoke a reaction that would spark the desperately needed rebellion. Their names escaped him, as did their faces, but the sounds of the gunshots didn't. None of the books in the library had the answer to whom, exactly, the protesters were, and every revolutionary tried to claim someone in their family was one of the murdered. He could never know their names for sure. You couldn't trust anyone in a place like this.

"It's lovely Ed," Oliver remarked.

"Thanks," Edward said, starting to pace back and forth in front of Oliver's desk, "it was so difficult to line up with all the children darting about. I took over eighty pictures before I snapped one that didn't have a blurry kid in it. I am kind of disappointed about the lack of color though. Makes it look too solemn. My next goal is to get them to use a photo for one of the posters that are going up all the time. Then I'll have truly made a name for myself around here. What do..."

"Ed," Oliver interjected, "I'm thinking about starting my own pamphlet."

"Neat," Edward said with enthusiasm, "not to sound

discouraging, but I don't know what you'd write about since the weekly report already provides everything that truly needs knowing. It would be an act of pure redundancy."

"I suppose you're right," Oliver replied with a sigh.

Oliver racked his brain for a subject that was just as worthy of being written about as the current revolution and he came up with nothing. The struggle touched everyone in a way that all other subjects didn't. There would be nothing preventing a potential pamphlet reader from ignoring him completely due to lack of interest, or preferring the leader's words over his own. It was the likely outcome if he ever did start up his own column. The fight was all anyone cared about, and was what all reasonable people should've cared about. His words would end up like all of the books in the room he spent most of his existence tending to. Unread and unimportant. He wasn't sure what to express in his nonexistent publication anyhow. There was no shortage of revolutionaries expressing intense loathing for the Vigil nor was optimism about the rebellion lacking in public discourse. He flipped the pamphlet over to look at the satirical cartoon on the back. It was a black and white drawing of a scorpion sporting a dunce cap, and it had a *V* for a stinger. It was piercing it through a human brain with the caption: "That'll fix it."

Out of the corner of his eye Oliver saw a crowd forming in Circle Park through one of the small windows.

"I didn't realize he was giving a speech today," Oliver said, rising from his desk and moving closer to the window for a better view.

Edward's eyebrows shot upwards, "we need to get

out there!" He burst through the library doors, savagely racing to get within earshot of the commotion.

Oliver hurried after him. He was knocked around by the throng of eager listeners clawing their way to the tree in the center of Circle Park. The waves of people crashed into him over and over again, and he wasn't quick enough to keep with the crowd and avoid getting trampled. Edward had already stepped over a few stragglers in an effort to get as close as he could.

Oliver ducked into an alleyway to avoid the onslaught of Insurrection uniforms piling into Circle Park. The standard Insurrection uniform consisted of a brown coat that hung down to the middle thigh. Along the back of the coat was a red symbol in the shape of a torch. It wasn't mandatory that anyone wear them, but everyone wore them when they were outside anyway out of pride.

Every face in the stampede was a typhoon of emotion. The younger folk bared their teeth in a distorted open smile as a few stray tears dripped down their cheeks. In their minds, Victory was the only reason such a speech would be called in the first place and they could finally celebrate in triumph. A few of them were waving their pamphlets in the air as they stormed forward. The older men and women held stern expressions as their eyes misted over, either that or they wailed in piercing agony. To his surprise, Oliver felt a droplet form in his eye, he was also crying in anticipation.

What could this possibly be about?

He glanced down at his carved hand again and began gritting his teeth. Maybe the day had come? A couple of minutes passed and the steady flow of Insurrection supporters slowed to a trickle. Oliver emerged from the alleyway and rushed as quickly as he could to hear what Nicholas had to say. Edward revealed himself from within the throng of listeners, grabbed Oliver by the wrist, and pulled him into the crowd. They both squirmed their way to the front despite the looks of contempt from the other attendees. Edward fumbled with the old Polaroid camera wrapped around his neck.

"Hello poster shot," Oliver heard Edward mumble. Nicholas was standing directly under the tree, his arms clasped behind his back, his legs locked, his eyes surveying the oncoming crowd. Oliver noticed that he had dyed his hair recently, getting rid of the gray gradient forming on the sides of his head. He was waiting for the last few to flow in.

Nicholas unsheathed his megaphone. All excitable chatter ceased almost immediately and the sea of people started listening intently. The crisp sting of megaphone feedback pierced Oliver's ears so badly that he had to cover them for the first few moments of the announcement, but eventually he grew used to the volume. He looked up with what felt like uncontrollable child-like wonder as Nicholas began speaking.

"It will not come as a surprise to any of you that The Vigil is brutally attempting to starve us out of our territory," Nicholas roared. His statement was met with widespread hissing and scoffing from the crowd.

"Over the course of two weeks they have sabotaged our underground supply lines which have been keeping us, and our children, alive throughout this revolutionary endeavor. We lost a lot of good men during these attacks, and now we are left with the difficult question of how we are going to feed ourselves. Despite what has been shown in the areas The Vigil still torments, we are certainly not a few weeks away from having our reserves depleted. However, we cannot let this injury go unanswered. We've shown numerous acts of mercy towards their troops and civilians, yet they cannot give us the courtesy of allowing us to feed our children!"

Some people began jumping, screaming, and demanding vengeance for the callousness inflicted on them by The Vigil. One person shouted, "kill the bastards!"

As the speech went on the expressions on the face of the mass contorted from sadness, anger, to unbridled joy without any visible intervening stage. Nicholas' eyes instructed the audience as to what the next emotion felt would be, and they responded correctly every single time. It was like watching a play, and Oliver could hardly resist the overbearing temptation to join in the revelry. He could feel himself burning with contempt for The Vigil, then transitioning to near crippling pity for the children of the Insurrection, moving into an overpowering feeling of joy knowing that the obstacle will soon be overcome. Nicholas told Oliver's emotions what to do, and he quite readily obliged.

Nicholas continued, "We will no longer stand by and allow this to happen. So, I am officially enacting the Emergency Protocol. In a pamphlet, to be delivered and released this afternoon, will be a list of the Insurrection Members being called to pick up a weapon and avenge this travesty inflicted upon us. We will show them that while they may be able to cow *their* population into subservice, they cannot destroy the spirit of freedom that burns within us! They must learn that their aggression is not water which puts out our flame. It is gasoline that will spread the purifying fire of justice until its tongues lash the deserving backs of those that seek to stamp it out!"

The crowd was insatiable and in violent agreement. It wasn't often that one was called lately, but Oliver remembered how often the Protocol was activated back when he first joined the Insurrection. He couldn't stop himself from shaking with a combination of rage and fear. Playing the entirety of his emotions off on rage was the safer option if his public image was to remain relatively unsullied. A willingness to die for the cause was necessary if this war was to be successful, but no one ever imagined themselves doing it. Yet, it's what everyone was currently clamoring to do. Did anyone else feel this fear? Was he the only one afraid of death? Was everyone else void of this concern, or did they merely refuse to express it? He could never know the answer to this question. None of the people in the crowd would ever know his true feelings either. No one could.

Edward lowered the camera from in front of his face. The expression on his face was miles different from Oliver's and the rest of the crowd. His mouth was slightly ajar, his eyes were wide, sweat everywhere, and his hands were shaking violently. Edward wasn't built for combat, neither was Oliver. They both knew that, but the Emergency Protocol did not distinguish by that metric. No one knew by what standard the Protocol chose Insurrection members to send to the front line. What everyone did know was Nicholas was the only one allowed to officially enact the policy.

Edward lost what little color was left in his face, dropped to the ground, and began gagging, clearly unable to deal with the gravity of the situation. Oliver grabbed Edward by the elbow and hoisted him to his feet again. The crowd was still jumping and screaming as Nicholas rang out the occasional inspirational statement which kept a solid supply of enthusiasm radiating through the audience. Gripping him tightly Oliver led Edward out of the crowd in order to give him some much needed space. The two men slipped into the alleyway that previously served as Oliver's hiding place. Their ears were still ringing from the torturous noise of the megaphone. Edward put his hands on his knees and started breathing heavily.

"Just relax," Oliver insisted as he patted Edward on his back, "deep breaths"

"I'm okay. Overly excited is all. Want to get back at those---" before he could finish his sentence Edward's gag reflex got the better of him, soiling the camera wrapped around his neck. Oliver rolled his eyes and kept comforting Edward.

"I swear if that shot's ruined I'm gonna be pissed," Edward chuckled, "when will the list be drawn up?"

"They have it drawn up already I'm sure. It should be getting here in a few hours. Go home, drink some water, meet me in my apartment after the surge at the library, and we'll read it together," said Oliver in a half-condescending tone.

"If you're not trampled to death first," Edward remarked with a snide grin as he departed towards the train station, wiping his mouth with the inside of his uniform sleeve.

CHAPTER TWO

FAINT SHADOWS OF RICKETY BUILDINGS LOOMED over the figure of Oliver like the branches of a dead willow. He was making his way back to the library to pick up the incoming pamphlet. Everything he set his eyes upon were stark reminders of what the world was, what they were, what he was, and the struggle. Some of the buildings had holes blown in them, and the owners had to use various scraps of wood to cover them in the winter time.

It was from when the fighting started, and a proper headquarters had yet to be established. Seeing the wounds inflicted on the walls of these structures reminded Oliver of the screams that would ring out after a bomb landed. There were promotional posters and graffiti strewn across the walls depicting the Torch of the Insurrection with Nicholas holding it. Oliver couldn't help but feel pride when looking at this artwork. To stand up to the Vigil was no easy feat when far fewer were committed to the cause.

Oliver then glanced down at his feet. His own

stride reminded him of the marching of soldiers being sent to the front when the Insurrection was lacking a proper number of armored vehicles. Sometimes they would march for miles without stopping, and then were forced to engage in combat without so much as a moment's rest. Not only did one have to die, but one had to die in the worst of conditions. Tired, hungry, sore, frightened, and forgotten about. They had to win.

Nothing could break Oliver's focus on the topic of the war against The Vigil. Every thought that he could muster could be connected to the fight. Oliver was not thoughtless; he simply had the same thought over and over again in different words. "We must defeat them." The word "win" pounded against the inside of his skull like a bass heavy battle drum with every step. "Win. Win. Win. Win." His mind was nothing more than a never ending repetition of a chant spoken in fancier terms. Unlike many others though, Oliver knew this about himself and he hated it.

The second he was resigning himself to his mental fate he had arrived at the library expecting an angry line of people desperate to see whether they were chosen, but no such line was there. Had the list already been delivered? From the alleyway Oliver could hear no commotion. It was oddly silent for such a large announcement.

Wrapping around to see if the package had been dropped off at its usual spot, Oliver saw no such package. Strips of thin plastic twitched on the ground due to the brisk breeze, some of them were getting stuck on the heftier specks of gravel that lined the side street. A faint grey layer of mist blanketed the ground and it was uncertain to Oliver as to whether it was exhaust or the result of the dust up caused by hordes of angry, excited, and frightened feet that pounded through here a short moment ago. Probably a bit of both. Fragments of names littered the ground. Not one of which was his or Edward's. Scattered patches of half-dead grass picketed the crevice between the gravel road and the buildings on either side of the cramped space.

He scoured the alley for traces of a pamphlet he could bring back to Edward. Eventually he found one buried in gravel. It was torn in several places and had dust outlines of boot prints on it, but it was still salvageable. Steeling himself not to jump at the opportunity to see if he or Edward were called upon, he shoved the pamphlet into his back pocket and made for the train station.

During his walk, he passed the old statehouse that had been liberated in the fighting. It was a magnificent structure. Leading up to the building that towered over the entirety of Insurrection territory was a set of pristine reflective granite steps. They were covered in coarse salt due to the imminent threat of losing one's footing on a sliver of ice. Above these steps were eight pillars. These pillars supported a front entryway, lined entirely by beautifully crafted stonework complete with carvings of ships, mythical creatures, and Great Men from History.

Oliver had no idea who these men were. No one did. Nor did any of them know the names of the mythical beasts depicted in the carvings. The roof consisted of a formidable red dome that was translucent when it came in contact with direct sunlight. The front double doors were the same gory color as the roof, and had two silver colored handles. Oliver only knew a few people who have seen the inside of the statehouse, and there was nothing exciting about it. Nothing but offices. It wasn't worth the time. Especially so, since the outside of the building was so gorgeous in comparison.

Oliver reached the train station just as his cheeks and fingertips began to sting in the frigid air. Shutting the glass door behind him blew up a couple shards of trash that lined the entrance. The urge to glance at the piece of paper that would ultimately decide his fate, and the fate of his closest friend, grew with each step.

Making his way down the steps to the underground platform, he weaved his way through a near endless stream of bums begging him for a scrap of food. Did any of them honestly think that he carried food around with him? It was as if they had already forgotten that there was a meat shortage reported today. Indeed, Oliver winged at what a selfish request it was considering the knife-edge the Insurrection was living on when it came to supplies of storable meat products. Their uniform jackets were stained permanently with dots of grease and various flavors of street grime. Nearly all of these souls threw themselves at Oliver in an attempt to get a scrap of sustenance. A few of them didn't notice Oliver was there, just staring into empty space, putting all of their mental effort into fusing themselves to the floor.

"Some food to spare?" one gaunt man wheezed.

"No, sorry," Oliver responded with a veneer of feigned regret.

Although in his mind Oliver was furious that he was being asked such a question in this trying time for the Insurrection. Everyone had to make sacrifices, and these men didn't appear to be making theirs in stride. After all, it wasn't Oliver's fault that they didn't have any food in their bellies, if it was even true that they were lacking food. He'd heard stories concerning these types of creatures. They would ask you for food, store it, and then take it home to their families so they had a larger ration. Men with bigger families did such things. Oliver couldn't tell whether his request was one of genuine need, or just an inconsiderate ploy to deprive him of his own supply of food. He could never tell.

As the bum shuffled out of Oliver's view the smell of the place hit his nostrils. It reeked of the corpses of worms after a heavy rain. He pulled the collar of his jacket over his nose to escape the abusive stench. Oliver peered over his shoulder as the train screeched to a halt in front of him. The doors slid open and Oliver stepped inside. The scent of the air evolved from nearly unbearable to a combination of leather and chemical cleaners.

His eyes adjusted to the harsh lights in the cabin. No seats were available. He steadied himself by grabbing one of the vertical metal bars near the doors right before the train lurched forward. He shut his eyes and tried to picture himself in another place, tightening his grip on the pole keeping him upright. The chatter filling the cabin was far too loud and varied to drown out completely, but Oliver was able to deafen the noise. His unconscious continually pounded the word "Win" against his temples.

"Now arriving at Block Seven," the automated voice said over the train's PA system. Oliver opened his eyes and saw a line accumulating to leave the train. This was his stop. He filed himself into the queue and exited in an orderly fashion.

People were shouting out their own names when he reached the surface again, waving the pamphlets in the air. Small groups of congratulators were forming around those who were chosen and they were asking all sorts of questions about what the operation would entail. The nervousness that enveloped him fueled his curiosity. He joined the small gathering around a young man wearing a uniform jacket that was far too big for him. The proud kid's sleeves would fall down to his elbows whenever he would dramatically lift the document that decided his near future, and they would conceal most of his hand when he swung his arms back down. His mouth was stuck in an enthusiastic open smile. He got to fight. He was needed somewhere. He was worth something. Oliver casually stepped through the gaggle surrounding this man. Oliver must've been around twice his age.

"What is the purpose of this Protocol? Where are you going, and what are you doing?"

"This is the final mission to be called. We're, at last, detonating a bomb in the center of where high-ranking Vigil members meet to discuss plans. You heard about the weapons testing?"

"Yes, but it said the weapons testing was a possibility."

"Possibility, yeah sure. The only reason we aren't given definitives is because the higher ups here don't want us in a panic. We know better."

"I didn't," Oliver said, pointing his eyes towards the ground.

"Now you do. Are you one of the called as well?" the boy asked with enthusiasm.

"I don't know," Oliver said dismissively as he walked away. He didn't bother to say goodbye as the boy had more questions to answer. It's not as if Oliver could trust his judgment anyhow.

Oliver climbed up the few steps in front of his apartment building. Only Oliver and Edward lived here. Edward lived in the downstairs apartment, but spent most of his time bothering Oliver with stupid questions and his generally incompetent demeanor.

They had been friends for as long as either of them could remember, and their relationship had a happy annoyance to it usually reserved for an older and much younger sibling.

Their building was an unstable looking thing despite being made almost entirely out of concrete. Unfortunately for Oliver, the blast of a grenade blew out one of his windows, and the wood he had used to board it up provided barely any insulation. He tried to block the daggers of cold wind with a couple of old blankets. They worked, but not close to completely. Shuffling up the thin metal steps to the wooden door that guarded his room, he heard the sound of someone messing with the knobs of the television.

Oliver opened the door and Edward was on his knees in front of the TV frantically trying to get the signal back grunting in frustration.

"Forget it!" Oliver said as he shut the door behind him, "If the damn thing loses picture it won't be back for at least another four hours."

Edward rose to his feet, "Let me read it!"

"Typical, not even a hello," Oliver said with a smirk

"Could say the same to you."

Oliver walked toward his doorless bathroom. He stopped at the sink and splashed lukewarm water on his face. Streaks of rust decorated the rim of the drain, and nearly every plumbing pipe was exposed. It was the same with the restrictively small shower wedged into the corner.

Edward slumped back into the navy blue recliner that sat in the middle of the two-room apartment. The television was still oozing a soft white noise. In the corner of the room near the blown out window was a disheveled pile of Insurrection pamphlets left to decay.

It reached Oliver's shoulder in height. Edward began to grow increasingly agitated.

"Do you think we're going to die?" Edward asked.

"We haven't even read the thing yet," Oliver replied.

"Yeah, but what about when we do?"

"What about it?"

"We can't survive out there. Look at us! Neither of us have any combat training, I barely know how a rifle functions, we don't even know what this mission is, I don't want us to..." Edward paused for a moment "I don't want us to fail."

"Nobody wants to fail, but if it's decided that we have to fight then we must. If no one showed up to fight when they were called The Vigil would plow right over us in a matter of days. I heard this is the final Protocol that will be issued though."

"Wonderful, probably means it's even more dangerous."

Oliver ignored the lightness in his chest, vibrating hands, and rapid heartbeat as he pulled the pamphlet out from his back pocket. He felt an invisible welt form in his throat and handed the pamphlet to Edward.

"Read it," Oliver said trying to make sure his voice didn't crack in the process.

"Okay," Edward said, snatching the pamphlet from Oliver's hand.

Edward began skimming through the list of names to himself. The television was still hissing at both of them.

"Well?" Oliver half-shouted in anticipation

"You've been called." Edward said.

"Let me see that!"

Oliver grabbed the pamphlet out of Edward's hand. He couldn't trust that Edward had read this correctly.

"And you?" Oliver asked

Edward looked up at Oliver and shook his head. While practically tearing the pages out after he turned them, Oliver examined the long list of strangers until he saw the precious ink that glared up at him.

"'*Oliver Walters*'" it read. In Section C Class B.

"'*All those called for Section C Class B. Report tomorrow morning at 0100 hours. Bring your weapons.*'"

"Edward, I need to get sleep. I leave tomorrow." Oliver said.

Edward rose from the chair and began pacing again.

"Maybe we could burn it, you know? Tear it into little pieces and burn it. They can't prove we saw the order, right? Maybe there weren't enough pamphlets for everyone and you couldn't have known to report for combat. I heard it was done before. If you really want to we can just pretend like we didn't see it!"

Oliver glanced up at Edward and stared at him until he calmed down a bit. Oliver did his best to seem calm, walked over to Edward, and embraced him.

"It's going to be alright, Ed. I'll miss you, but now we'll both be useful to some degree."

Edward stopped his furious pacing and moved toward the front door.

Edward smiled weakly and gave Oliver a reluctant salute before shutting the front door behind him. Oliver sat down in his recliner, fished in the cushion with his hand, and pulled out his only weapon. It was a grey-colored long barreled revolver. This firearm wasn't designed for someone with a slender build, but it was the only gun he had. The handle of the gun singed his hand with frigidity. He gripped it tighter in order to get used to the burn of the cold.

Oliver pointed the revolver at the television and envisioned a Vigil agent standing directly in front of him. The uniform slowly began to take form. The near perfectly round blue-grey helmet that engulfed most of the face, the sharp black *V* stenciled on the front, the hefty mish-mosh of defense padding that resembled a neglected laundry bin. The wide black belt. The wrinkled and ruffled pants. The ignorant confidence. The dripping contempt for the common man. A lust for death. The selective sociopathy. The boots tightened to a painful degree as if the goal was to replace one's flesh with leather and steel. The flesh was the last item to materialize in Oliver's mind. No face. No veins. Just a human shaped mass of pinkish tissue filled the uniform. He pulled the hammer back and pointed the gun directly at its head. His thumb began to shake due to the weight of the firearm. The critical finger twitched, but the click he was waiting for was drowned out by the wheezing screen.

CHAPTER THREE

THE GRINDING OF THE ENGINE AND THE SOUND OF small rocks being crushed by the rubber tires blended into one another. The rigidity of the truck bed dug into Oliver's backside. He uncomfortably rested his back against one of the thin metal frames used to hold a black tarp over the soldiers. There were around fifteen men compressed into this cramped jagged space. Most of them had cigarettes in their hands letting the ash carelessly fall to the ground like snowflakes in the dry air. A fight almost broke out when someone's ash blew into the eye of another passenger. Each inhalation was a miniature sunrise illuminating the faces of the men in a beautiful momentary orange and yellow gradient.

Oliver was being gently crushed by the two men at his sides. The one on his left was a mammoth of a man. At least six and a half feet in height and massive. He forced himself into an upright fetal position to free up space for the other passengers. The man on Oliver's right was rather average looking. There was nothing special or notable about him. He had a face that belonged in large crowds and nowhere else. It was a face one forgets immediately after seeing it. Short brown hair, thin lips, average build, average height, not particularly gaunt or chubby in the cheeks. He was clutching his sky-pointed rifle tightly and flecks of white and pink made themselves apparent in his knuckles.

It always got colder as one ventured out from the city. The miles long wasteland separating the city from the Divide was studded with craters that had frozen over. Scars of earth created by shellfire forced into permanence by the constant iciness of the air. They all tried to dress in a manner they thought would be conducive to winter combat though most of them made the decision to value warmth over readiness. Two men were wearing thick mittens. One was wearing a mask that was too large for him, obscuring part of his left eye. All of the men had their Insurrection uniform on as the outer layer.

A boy of about nineteen was clinging to the black tarp with one hand to prevent it from making noise and flapping around. In his other hand was a half-burnt cigarette. His eyes were near circular with fear. His hand was shaking so much that he had difficulty bringing his cigarette to his lips.

"Don't worry about him," the man sitting to his right said. "He's had six already." His voice was raspy and deep despite not having the build or face made for such a thing.

Oliver could barely hear him over the clanking of the truck.

"I always thought cigarettes were strange things. People use them to relax, but technically they're a stimulant," Oliver replied.

"Gives a man confidence when he's lacking it. You're overthinking. It's more a matter of repetition. Like a child sucking on a bottle. It's not necessarily what's inhaled it's the ritual of inhalation that relaxes people."

"Apart from the whole 'nicotine is addictive' thing?"

His smirk subsided, "Name's Reece."

"Oliver. Good to—"

"Save it," Reece said sharply as he stood up and steadied himself.

The man who had been chain smoking was turning a tinge of green with nausea. Reece screamed for the truck to stop. All of the makeshift soldiers looked at him in a confused stupor.

"Go relieve yourself," Reece said to the sick man.

The man stumbled out the back of the truck and they were all treated to an orchestra of heaving as Reece began to take command. His quiet deep raspy voice was overtaken by a frantic tenor.

"Trust has been placed in me to lead you through this. We will be taking a large stash of non-perishable rations from the Vigil tomorrow evening. It is my job to lead you to our stake-out position. Tomorrow evening is when we're going to steal it for ourselves. This particular small warehouse is located in a near abandoned town barely ten miles from the Divide. Unfortunately for them, they haven't been smart enough to move it. Any questions?"

"We stopped," the large man said.

"No shit," Reece snapped back, "we're walking from here so as to not arouse more suspicion than we need. The sound of this truck would attract the attention of every Vigil agent guarding the Divide. We're climbing it."

All of the men adapted themselves to the new power structure. There was no documentation of any kind proving that this guy was appointed to be in charge of the operation. Reece spoke with a roaring authority strong enough to make a pacifist draw a firearm. Even the most physically imposing man among the group was put in his place through the utterance of two syllables.

Oliver hopped out the back of the truck. The dirt and gravel crunched as he landed. The strength of the wind stung his face. Thousands of microscopic needles of cold pierced his pores. The dirt looked as close to concrete as nature would allow. About as tough a substance too. Only bombs or a complex process of freezing and thawing could penetrate it. Flat nothing-ness spanned in every direction. The driver of the van turned around and started driving back across his own tracks back toward safety.

"Extra mask?" Oliver asked out loud to the group of men standing around. He was mostly ignored. The eyes of the men who did turn their heads were filled with mockery and contempt. After a short conversation with the driver Reece ordered the men to march east. There was no way Oliver's nose would survive this journey without turning black. He could already feel his tear ducts crystallizing.

He marched forward in the middle of the other men. Their bodies barely held back the painful temper-ature of the wind. He lifted his left arm and buried his nose and mouth into his elbow. Saving his nose and lips were first priority. His eyes could manage by being slammed shut for a few minutes as he walked forward. Everyone was moving in the same direction anyhow. Reece seemed completely unaffected by the conditions. It looked as if he was taking a stroll on a peaceful spring afternoon, with the Divide becoming more visible with each strained step.

Oliver's thighs and feet began burning a couple hours into the march. A hot pulsing pain bombarded the left side of his abdomen as well. He was reluctant to wish the pain away because it was a distraction from the stabbing cold. The ache became so unbearable that he had to put his arm down for a few minutes at a time surrendering his most vulnerable skin to the elements. He repeated the phrase "three more steps" in his head, saying one word per footstep to try and pass the time and ignore his surroundings. When this stopped working he resorted to saying it out loud, but had to stop because his breath fogged up his glasses rendering him even blinder than he already was.

His eyes slammed shut once again to melt the ice forming around them. He began to miss his library work. No, this was for victory. He looked forward to relaying this horrific story to Edward. A journal jostled around in his backpack. The first entry, he decided, would be about this weather and how during the brief pockets of still air the pain would intensify as the cold no longer numbed the nerves. If the journal was for any purpose it was so he could turn his life into something tangible and History could be absolutely sure he existed.

Reece stopped abruptly and Oliver bumped into the man in front of him. They were finally approaching the Divide. It spanned beyond sight in either direction. A stone wall that acted as bone crawling through the flesh of the Earth itself. It was about two men in height and a darker grey than the rest of the world. Spotlights on the left and right sides of their position became visible. Reece had calculated the location perfectly so they were directly in the middle of two spotlights perched just behind the Divide. Territorial control over the Divide was paramount in the war, and each side was constantly taking and relinquishing control over certain sections of it. Although the Vigil occupied most of it at that point.

As they grew closer the details of the bricks became more prominent. This was not a structure built through the whirring of engines. Each stone looked as if it was placed personally and haphazardly. Some weren't more than pebbles while others were borderline boulders. Thick mortar filled even the largest gaps between the individual stones and despite the careless nature of the stone placement the Divide was one of the most structurally sound buildings Oliver had ever seen. The stones were shaved down on either side to create a consistent thickness throughout the face of the Divide.

He remembered stories of this beast from his childhood friends. He was told that it was so immense even the sky was replaced with it; that the shadow it cast extended only one mile from their own fortifications. These tales were untrue, but it didn't stop Oliver from fearing it just the same. With every pulse of desire to tear it down stone by stone it grew larger and sturdier in his mind. It was as if it had been there since the Earth was born. Oliver was certain they could scale it. There was no barbed wire adorning the top of the wall which he thought was a huge oversight. What kind of impervious structure allowed for two men to render it useless in its function?

Reece pressed his back against the Divide's face and hysterically waved his arms gesturing for everyone to join him. He pointed at the team's colossus of a man and then pointed towards the sky. The large man clasped his hands together, bent his knees, and steadied himself against the wall. One by one the men were launched over the Divide. Oliver was one of the first over. While struggling to haul himself up he caught a glimpse of the landscape. Rocks studded the ground like scattered uneven rivets. There were a few trees spending all of their energy trying to remain vertical, stripped of everything but their skeletons. No stars. Too many dark clouds cloaked the area for that. The moon was visible as a tinge of light grey barely forcing itself to the surface. No wildlife. No movement apart from the men who had already reached the other side, the men operating the spotlights, and whatever the wind decided to toss around. If this area was anything before the war began it was lost to History.

He imagined a bustling city filled with optimistic artists and opportunistic taxi drivers trying their hardest to pick up rich clients. This image morphed into a picturesque farming town where the roads were studded with long tan grass, the sky bore amusing cloud formations, and the trees were a bright and saturated green. Places where hope oozed out of every pore. There would always be a sinister side to life but at least it was hidden then. The world looked like it had given up and flipped onto its back. Every temperamental toddler, every slick lying salesman, every uncaring hypocrite, every petty club woman, every insecure bully, every dribbling power-hungry politician, every bigot, every hate-filled self-interested lowlife had been introduced to the searing light. Instead of sizzling away they became emboldened by it. They fed on it like gluttons, draining the radiance from every secluded crevice that tried to rekindle it, and then wondered to themselves with dumbfounded curiosity where all the warmth had gone.

A dim yellow glow flickered in the distance leaking out of a city. It was pleasant, and provided some color to the surrounding emptiness. He couldn't help but appreciate it.

He landed on the other side. Reece was right behind him. Ten men made it over the Divide before the screaming started. The large man had thrown the young sick man over the wall with too much force. Arms and legs flailing like a pinwheel he smashed into the frozen ground and wailed, clutching his left bicep. His radial bone was sticking out of his forearm and his flesh flopped around like a human flagpole. Reece ordered everyone to run immediately. The spotlights turned on the squad of men. Oliver turned away and sprinted forward trying to keep close to Reece. The cracking of gunfire replaced the young man's screeching.

"They killed him!" one man shouted.

No one answered his yelping. They were too busy trying to keep traction on frozen dirt with hole-filled boots. The men operating the spotlights began firing wildly in the direction Oliver was running. One bullet whizzed by his right leg, around two inches from where his foot was. Two men were injured during the retreat. Oliver tried to get the others to help carry them, but they all kept sprinting. The torches on their uniforms were getting smaller and smaller. He had to keep running or he would be stranded in this god-forsaken place.

"Don't you go with them!" an injured man grabbed a handful of Oliver's uniform jacket.

"Let go! I have to, I'm sorry." Oliver said frantically

"No you don't they'll execute me out here, you maniac!"

"I don't have time to reason with you. They'll kill me!"

"They'll kill *me*, you worthless shit!"

The man's eyebrows were sharp and pointed toward the bridge of his nose. He was shrieking his words through his teeth. Oliver eventually had to stomp on the man's wound to wrestle out of his grasp. The man yelped in betrayed pain like a loving puppy that just got a face full of his owner's foot.

Oliver continued to run trying desperately to catch up with the rest of the group after scrambling out of reach. Looking behind him, the injured man's face contorted from optimistic anger to hopeless acceptance. The eyebrows were now pointed toward the hairline almost leaning against one another. This was the first time Oliver had witnessed someone so resigned to death. He always imagined his first experience with death would be in triumphant celebration over removing evil from the comforts of life with righteous rage.

Suppressing his nausea, Oliver caught up with the rest of the group and none of them noticed his return. He thought of the men left behind the Divide and knew there was no possible way they would be found. Their only choice was to circle back and try to make it somewhere warm before the freezing temperatures sucked the life out of them. Either that or they were shot too. The walk back was far too long to presume their survival. Every step towards victory cost a body or two. While discouraging, Oliver couldn't let it get to him.

The bodies would diffuse the worry of the Vigil. After all they were unsure of how large a force they were and fired off into the gamble of the darkness. Once the frozen corpses are discovered they'll assume they've weakened the squad past the point of possible success. In a sense, it was fortuitous that they had been shot. Oliver tried to scold himself for wanting to save the injured man in the first place, but couldn't bring himself to do it. Which was worse? Condemning a man to death through the euphoria of hypothermia and a few quick gunshots, or forcing him to continue living this kind of wretched life? There was no time to think about this question now, nor was there time then.

CHAPTER FOUR

As they approached the outskirts of the city, excitement and paranoia began to bubble among the men left alive. Oliver couldn't feel his face or fingers anymore so he kept the talking to a minimum. He was worried that he was so brittle that moving his lips would cause his skin to split. The men with masks on began speaking in short muffled questions about details that none of them knew, and were only asked as catharsis for an overworked adrenaline gland. Despite the cold Oliver's head was pouring sweat. It pooled in his clothing and the frost made the damp sections rigid.

The warehouse had the same look and feel of nearly everything else. It was three stories high and made of cracked concrete. It was completely surrounded by a chain link fence. The only color on the building was a faded light blue that covered the bits of the roof that were triangular and jutting out from the third story. The rest of the roof was completely flat. All of the windows were boarded up. Moving towards the building Reece began to walk slower and with more care about keeping noise to a minimum. The remaining men followed suit without having to have an order barked at them.

Once the exhausted group reached the fence Oliver leaned on it, shoving his head into his forearm, desperate to get some rest, but Reece instantly swerved his eyes to meet Oliver's the moment he heard the rattling. There was no barbed wire preventing people from climbing over, but there were the sharp ends of metal wires to deal with.

Reece took off his uniform jacket and threw it so it covered the loose sharp metal weeds shooting out from the top of the fence. He climbed over the fence and motioned for the rest of the group to do the same, and it was done without too much hassle except for one of the men who got a nasty gash on his palm for screwing up his initial attempt at jumping onto the fence. He wrapped the wound up using one of his socks.

Reece tore away loose bricks that were blocking a small window into the basement, and one by one they all made their way inside. The endless thrashing of the skin by the frosty wind had finally stopped. Oliver took his gloves off, shoved them in his pocket, and started rubbing his cheeks trying to get some friction going. He wiped his mouth and found that his lip had indeed split and was bleeding a little. He pulled his uniform sleeve over his hand and put pressure on his mouth as everyone ascended the metal staircase to the top floor.

Holes in the concrete walls exposed the maws of pipes that were drooling rust. Oliver had an unexplainable wish to see a rat, or some living creature, peek its face out and then retreat back into one of those tunnels. Animals have survived in crueler colds than this. He just wanted to see something with a disinterested look in its eye.

Oliver climbed the last flight of stairs. The third floor was devoid of furniture and machinery. Debris piled up in the corners. The place excreted a smell as if spray paint went rancid and had mold sprouting from it. Oliver's face clenched when the odor slammed into his face. Many of the other men did as well. Reece took his pack off and everyone, with a collective relieved sigh, did the same. They started scraping at the floor with their boots trying to clear the grime aside so they could sit down. A couple of them gave up and sat on their backpacks. How many were left? He counted eight including himself. Reece was sitting alone staring into middle space. Clearly his mind was occupied. Oliver sat in the circle with everyone focusing on his own hands, taking his gloves off and fidgeting with them, trying to rewarm them.

"Let's get a small fire going," one man said as he took a book of matches and some oil out of his pack. Oliver still had his pamphlet crumpled up in the back pocket of his only pair of pants. Many of the other men had scraps of paper and lint to throw in. It wasn't enough for an enormous sustainable fire, but it should make the place a bit warmer for a little while. The man dumped some oil on the kindling and lit the match. Oliver immediately felt relief on the tip of his nose and eyebrows and closed his eyes, soaking in the small bit of heat and light they had. The men were mesmerized by the fire for a few minutes until the silence was broken.

"It's bullshit," one of the men said, "They're honestly trying to starve us out huh?"

"They made me tell my kids that they had to eat

half-rations so we could store something if this whole thing keeps up," another man replied.

"But think about what that means! They're fine with letting our children starve just so they can ruin us. I'm telling you, these people have no conscience. All they see is the jacket. Let that sink in for a second."

"It's all selective and hypocrisy. If we tried starving their kids they'd be all over it. Printing up a whole bunch of shit about how we love to kill kids. It's okay when *they* do it though."

"No sense of decency, I'd like to see one of their kids starving and see how they like it."

Laughter exploded out of the men, "Yeah, yeah show 'em what it feels like. Then maybe they'd knock it off. I hope we take this food right out of their mouths."

Through hearty chuckles one man said, "You think any of these bastards know which hole to put the food in?"

The laughter grew stronger. Oliver participated in conversations like this daily. He smirked and started laughing through his nose. He then chimed in and said, "Of course they don't, they need published instructions for eating hanging in the kitchen so they don't forget."

The laughter grew even louder and soon a few of the men were crying with joy. Oliver kept his mouth covered to keep the noise down. He glanced over at Reece. He looked like someone trying to handle a complex math problem in his head. He was sitting down, but leaning forward. His lips were pursed, his brow furrowed, his eyes were darting about, and he was staring at nothing but the flickering wall which was studded with grayed out and shattered windows at the other end of the room. Nobody was paying attention to him. They were all too busy laughing.

Oliver felt he knew all of them intimately now because on some level he was them. A small group of shunned people, outlaws, the boogeymen of the Vigil's collective unconscious. All sitting together around a bootleg fire exchanging stories of triumph and misery without a care in world whether the tales were true. Even though there existed a world that hated them for the mere act of being, in this one place, there was some solace from it. It was necessary in a time like this to be ruthless. Any inkling of "Golden Rule" talk had been chipped away from common conversation, and how an eye for an eye makes the whole world blind or the biggest lie of all: *Treat others the way you wish to be treated.* All a cover for cowards and fools. Oliver couldn't count how many eyes the Vigil had taken, nor how many times it treated the Insurrection in horrible ways that they wouldn't want brought upon themselves. Nicholas had refuted the whole thing in just two sentences of a long opinion piece of his called The Philosophy of Advantage:

"An eye for an eye doesn't make the whole world blind. It levels the playing field."

All of the impartiality had been ejected from the institutions and this led everyone down one of two paths. Everything else was walled off, dejected and cowardly. Every "association" and "organization" was subject to this fracturing aside from the political ones. Less and less care was given to maintaining any sort of objective means of examination. Every act of partiality and violence justified further acts of partiality and violence. Something had to give way, and it did. Volunteers for polling stations began fudging the numbers. This provoked an inevitable retaliation and thus began a complete collapse of trust in the democratic process.

There were wayward bombings and acts of cruelty that fierce politicians began endorsing. In reacting to these endorsements more extreme measures were taken by policy-makers, which just made it all the more tempting to shoot the politicians advocating these terrible measures in the chests.

It took multiple decades to chip away the idea that there were lines one should never cross. Effectiveness was all that mattered eventually. Even the most stoic of people got sucked into the storm. Either that or they were killed. Every oath was treated literally as if they were "just words" and every contract and treaty was treated like "just a piece of meaningless paper."

The disgust that came from looking at an opponent's face became too much to bear and it all collapsed. The whole damned thing. Generals, politicians, criminals, soldiers, police officers, teachers, scholars, musicians, lawyers, writers, comedians, all the way to bartenders, construction workers and maids were split in two over who started it. The only agreement that could be reached between them was that one of them had. There *had* to be a way to confirm that the Insurrection wasn't the aggressor here. Maybe that'd be the first step in stopping this fighting? Truth! An advantageous truth no less. All Oliver wanted to do was win and stop the fighting. Goodness knows the Vigil wouldn't listen to the truth. As if they ever did.

It was like a nightmare, but an exciting nightmare where instead of waking up and screaming until the lungs burst, the monster could be defeated and one could retire to bed with its bloodied head sitting pretty on the nightstand. A huge fissure cracked through the middle of the country. On one side were people who cared so much they couldn't tell the difference between

murder and leaving a lousy tip when making judg-
ments. On the other, people who cared so little that
things which didn't affect them might as well have
never happened at all as they happily held hands with
the most fiendish of men. Everybody else was dead and
gone.

"We're about a hundred twenty-five yards from
them. Put the fire out." Reece ordered.

A couple of the men groaned.

"You're lucky I let it go at all, put it out." Reece
shouted

Two of the men stomped the fire out as best they
could. Some of the ash was still smoldering on the
concrete floor.

"Oliver, you'll stay awake with me to keep an eye
out. Brace yourself." Reece said.

Oliver shut his eyes, audibly sighed, and bit down
so hard he could've sworn a tooth cracked.

"Okay," Oliver said.

His eyes already felt like lead weights, his stomach
had the feeling of being empty and uncomfortably full
at the same time. Every twitch of the limbs had to be
mentally prepared for. He wasn't ready for this job. He
needed sleep, but the sun was rising and he pleaded
with his body for a second wind. As the other men
huddled together in the corner near the dead flame,
using their jackets as both padding underneath and
blankets on top, Reece tossed Oliver a pair of
binoculars.

"I don't know if I can stay awake for this job, does it
have to be me?" Oliver asked

"Are any of the men less tired?" Reece turned
towards the group. "Hey, do any of you think you can
stay awake for another eight hours?"

"No," the men said in near unison.

"Any other objections?" Reece asked.

"No, fine."

Reece pried out one side of one of the boards in the window so that they could see through it. Oliver looked through the binoculars and saw a small building that looked like it was once a convenience store. The walls were not much more than large windows, and there were about five men in view. Occasionally one of the men would go into a back room with rations, and come out a few minutes later empty handed.

What they doing in there? Who is back there that needs feeding? Why aren't they out in the open with the others? Do they have a prisoner? All questions that went through Oliver's mind.

"Alright, you take other side." Reece ordered

"Okay," Oliver said.

He walked over to the other side of the room to a window that had a thin gap between planks of wood that he could see through. He looked through the slit. Nothing but dirt, dark sky, and a fuzzy ball of white where the moon was struggling through the clouds. He grabbed his journal, then sat back down and started to write. But where to start? Yes, the weather:

"Forgetting to bring a mask was my first mistake. Lots of wind. The ground has hardly any give to it. I don't think that my nose and lips will ever recover from how frigid it is outside of the cities. Met one man named Reece. I don't know the names of any of the others. Didn't bother to ask. I let a good man die because I was afraid..."

Oliver had to look up from the last sentence. He was trying not to believe it. No, obviously he had let him die because trying to save him would've been advantageous for the Vigil. They would've caught them much easier, maybe killed even more of them. In being injured he'd become a burden, a liability. Those justifications weren't convincing him, despite how many times he repeated them to himself. He'd experienced that fear in the moment. He remembered it. He wasn't thinking strategically at the time. He had only been concerned about his own safety and it made him ashamed.

"Writing?" Reece asked

Oliver instinctively flinched, slammed the journal shut and tried to hide it.

"Um, just a little. For a friend of mine. He didn't get called up and he wanted to know what it was like out here. I'm mostly talking about how cold it is."

"Mostly?" Reece asked

"Yeah.."

"You work at the library don't you?"

"Yes.."

"Have you ever read any of those books?"

"Not in a long time. I used to read books, but it just seemed pointless as time went on. Too focused on other things."

"Do you read the Weekly Report?"

"Well sure, everyone does. It's the only way to keep up to date on things," Oliver said as a smile grew on his face, "my favorite piece was when Nicholas wrote his refutation of the 'eye for an eye' stuff. It changed my life."

"Mmm, mine too," Reece said. "What do you think of the Vigil's pamphlets?"

"Propaganda," Oliver said instantly.

"See, when you think propaganda you think lies right? Lies aren't all that's needed. Lies can be disproven. All you need to do is appeal to the right thing." Reece said.

Oliver moved closer to him and started listening intently. He heard shades of Nicholas in his cadence.

Reece continued with the condescending yet upbeat tone of a salesman, "Propaganda depends on the person or group being convinced. Are they sensitive? Tug at their heartstrings. Are they hard-hearted and gruff? Appeal to their sense of justice or logic. Are they fearful? Be fearless. Are they uncertain? Be certain. Most are close-minded so appealing to their innate fears and worries works wonders, but it can be difficult when you need them to move beyond those innate fears and worries. The open-minded are slightly easier because all you need is a decent enough argument. If they are stubborn enough to rebuff all of your advances you can accuse them of being an ideologue who isn't open to progress. They can convince any man to do anything under the right circumstances. I've studied this for a while now."

"That's why we put out the report. To counter their propaganda," Oliver said.

Reece took a sharp breath in, held it for a moment, and sighed, "precisely."

Both of them went back to their posts and were silent for around ten minutes.

Reece then asked, "Oliver, would you lie about anything if it benefitted the Insurrection?"

"Yes," Oliver said.

"Good," Reece replied.

"I'd do anything to end this war as quickly as possible," Oliver said.

"Me too."

Another ten minutes of silence.

"Nicholas is getting too old. He's grown too tender and he's going to lose us this war. I guarantee it," Reece said.

Oliver didn't answer for a few moments for fear it was a test of loyalty. Reece needed people for the raid. It would be disadvantageous to the cause to kill him for merely being uncertain.

"He gives us someone to rally behind," was all Oliver could think to say.

"Exactly, the man's a vessel. A conduit. The human equivalent of a radio antenna. Swap him out for any other lowlife with decent oratory skills and no one would ever know the difference."

Oliver was getting angry.

"Is this some kind of test? A joke?"

"God damn, listen to you. What matters here? What's the one thing that everyone wants?"

"For the war to end in victory."

"Right, now if there was a person actively hindering that end should we continue allowing them to lead us?"

"No."

"That's all I'm trying to get across. Nicholas has you so wrapped up in *him* that you've forgotten the central goal here, the philosophy that has gotten us this far. Advantage. We can't be fussing around with things like loyalty or hero worship if they're not helping us."

"What if they do help?"

Reece sighed, "Then by all means."

Another few minutes of silence went by. He couldn't help but think Reece had a point. There hadn't seemed to be any major progress in years, and people were becoming complacent. All they seemed to concern themselves with was the Weekly Report and being there for one of the speeches. The figure of Nicholas isn't what everyone was fighting for after all. He was just the human manifestation of it. Not much reflection was needed to convince Oliver that the choice between Nicholas and Victory was clear.

"The most difficult task for the propagandist to perform, Oliver, is to condemn with full honesty the cruelty that his enemies display and then, with full honesty, find that very same cruelty an unfortunate necessity when he performs it himself. Once he reaches that stage of enlightenment there is nothing that he can't accomplish." said Reece.

"Why are you telling me this?" Oliver asked.

"Because you were writing something and didn't want me to know what it was," Reece replied.

They sat there for hours saying absolutely nothing after that, with quiet wind and snoring men in their ears. For the rest of the night, whenever Oliver's mind got hungry, it would gnaw at the tendons that connected the righteous and the necessary and at the question of whether all of this was.

CHAPTER FIVE

DAY BROKE. AT THIS POINT OLIVER HAD BEEN awake for two straight days and he was reaching the moment where his body became entirely mechanical. He had to put all of his energy into the basics of moving and speech. On multiple occasions throughout the night he caught himself on the verge of sleep and jolted upright again, keeping an eye on an empty flat stretch of dead land. Reece began clapping.

"Alright boys, up, up!" Reece shouted

All of the sleeping men rustled around for a few seconds, then stood upright, brushed off their jackets, and put them back on. Oliver struggled to get to his feet. What he wouldn't give to wrap his hands around a warm mug of coffee right about now. Just inhaling the hot steam and light bitter aroma would be enough to satisfy him for a couple of hours. The image of the still landscape was imprinted in Oliver's vision. Whenever he would rub his bloodshot eyes he could've sworn he saw the shining residue from the moon glistening behind his eyelids.

"Hey, how're we getting outta here?" one man asked.

"What?" Reece said.

"Are we gunna have to carry all that food?"

"For a little while."

"You kidding me? Where am I gunna put all the shit I brought?"

"Relax, I'm trying to count. Figure it out."

The men grumbled to themselves and started arguing about which canned foods were the heaviest and how to best evenly distribute the weight. They came to the conclusion that canned sauces were the heaviest due to the lack of air within the can itself. Oliver walked away from his post, fighting against the desire to wallow in self-pity over his present and future fatigue. He took a knee beside the group of men looking for a way to get a fire going again. The only thing Oliver had to contribute was a small strip of fabric he ripped from the damaged hem at the bottom of his pant leg. Eventually they got a fire going again. The oldest man in the group was fidgeting around and making guttural sounds of annoyance.

"Did any of you ever think you'd be carrying cans of food when you joined up?" He asked the group.

"Nope, but we gotta eat," another man interjected

"Yeah, I suppose."

"When *did* you defect anyway?" Oliver asked him.

"Ah, about two years ago I think."

"You might be the newest recruit here," Oliver said as he smiled.

"Probably am. Took me a while to decide on because of my family."

"It must have been difficult getting them all out of there."

The older man rubbed his forehead and shut his eyes. He looked back up again.

"I didn't."

"Why not?"

"Wife didn't agree with me. Had a big blowout fight about it. I was so angry that she was willing to take the Vigil's nonsense day in and day out. I'd been growing out of the bullshit they fed us every day. I knew they had been lying. Law after goddamn law making it harder and harder to do anything worthwhile. We'd just had a baby and she wanted to make the tattooing appointment. I begged her not to do it. She forced it on them anyway. That night I carved off my tattoo in the bathroom, and tacked a note on the inside of the front door saying that I was leaving for good. It probably hurt her and the kids. She didn't understand that I cared about the kids too and wanted them to live in a world where they don't have to worry about all this. Now I've been tasked with stealing food from them."

"You're doing the right thing," another man counseled.

"Eh, she probably wants me dead by now. If my child grows up he'll want me dead too. She'll pass it off as a betrayal, and why shouldn't she? It's a real shame she made them stay. The kids didn't understand what was going on or what was at stake here."

"What happened to her?" one of the men asked.

"Don't know. All I know is that she guaranteed that my children will be evil and I can't forgive her for that," the older man said as he looked towards the fire. "They'll be put through *their* schools and makes friends with *other* Vigil children. They'll be brainwashed beyond recognition and they won't consider me their father anymore. They'll be mindless and angry. I'll just be another enemy drone. They'd try to kill me if they ever see me again. That bitch."

"They kill people over there who don't have the tattoo, right?"

"Wouldn't put it past them. I've heard about it happening."

"Kinda weird she'd want your kids in a place where they'd kill ya over a dumb tattoo."

"Yeah very."

Oliver had a family once. His father was a very prim and snooty man. The same basic routine had to be followed every single dawn for him. Wake up at 6:45 AM, tell Oliver to brew the coffee, read the government's daily leaflet, eat breakfast, then go to work as a military bureaucrat. They wouldn't let him fight due to his bad knee joints. It was very important not to disturb this morning routine or he would get frustrated. The most vivid memory of his father was the wrinkle in his forehead whenever he would raise his eyebrows. With his mother though, it had to be the way her cheeks ballooned whenever she smiled. Oliver couldn't remember what she did for a living, but imagined her as a nurse. When Oliver was very young he would make silly faces to make her laugh and he adored seeing her smile wide and bright. He couldn't remember their voices. He had voices for them in his head. His father's voice was very gruff and deep, while his mother's was light and warm. Despite his best efforts he knew that he'd manufactured these voices after being away from them for decades. If anything, he wanted to hear them again so he could accurately disprove his memory.

The men began playing cards around the fire, sometimes shouting accusations of cheating at one another. They weren't betting anything worthwhile, they just wanted to see which one was the best at the game. Oliver decided not to participate, he leaned against the window of his previous post. Reece was still mumbling to himself and looking through his binoculars. Oliver desperately wanted to talk to him again. There was something about him that seemed momentous and historic. The immediate world seemed to have no effect on him. He brushed off complaints from the men, pushed himself through walls of frigid air, and dealt with death the same way one dealt with losing a single hair off of their head.

His mind was so full there was no room for uncertainty. Oliver was jealous of that. Reece didn't even fear throwing an unkind word in the direction of Nicholas if he felt the need to. Reece wanted to tell him about his misgivings, and it made Oliver feel a step above the rest of the men. He liked this feeling. His body took over and forced him into a near immediate deep sleep with the image of Reece burnt into his eyes.

"Wake up!" Reece shouted as he shook Oliver by his jacket's lapel.

"What! What's happening?" The sun was down now.

"Good, you're awake. You needed that."

"I'm sorry, I don't know what happened. How did I let myself..."

"It's fine. Advantage my friend, remember? When the human body doesn't get sleep it gets delirious, your fine motor skills turn to mush, and you're useless to me as a soldier."

"Alright, alright" Oliver said, climbing down from his panic.

"Come here. I need to show you something."

Reece helped Oliver off of the ground and walked

over to the window he'd been staring out of for hours. They sat there in silence for a bit.

"There are nine of them," Reece said.

"They have the numbers on us," Oliver said.

"Barely. I need at least one person alive after this is all over."

"Okay. What about the food?"

"We'll figure it out, but I can't do it alone. You'll stay up here, and on my signal, shoot out one of their windows. Preferably one of the bigger ones, on the opposite side of the building to where we are for a diversion, and into one of their chests."

"I'm not the best shot here. I can guarantee it."

"That doesn't matter now. I need it to be you so you can help me after we get back to Insurrection territory."

"With what?"

"Who writes the Weekly Report?"

"Nicholas, of course."

"Wrong. It's me."

"You're lying"

"I'm not. I don't compile the basic information, but I assure you that I write all of the opinion pieces. Nicholas hired me specifically to do so."

"Prove it" Oliver whispered.

"Ha! Proof. Listen to you. Proof? When have you ever needed that before?"

Oliver began to get nervous, "What are you talking about?"

"You're demanding proof now because you don't *want* to believe me. You're still breaking out of this childish worship of a man you've never met. I wrote every single line of *The Philosophy of Advantage* and that's what you've always fawned over Nicholas for doing. Admit it."

Reece was right. It was like he could read his thoughts. Oliver believed him.

"Why me?" Oliver asked.

"Because you're wrestling with the same paradox I fought, and solved. Would you commit hypocrisy if it meant gaining an advantage over the Vigil?"

"Yes," Oliver said.

"Good, now, can you now condemn the Vigil for committing hypocrisies?"

"Sure" Oliver said with a bit of discomfort.

"You feel that? That slight pang of guilt? That tiny hesitation before answering? I've discovered a way to make that go away. I've learned how to kill self-awareness in people, although folks like us with the capacity to understand the process are resistant to its techniques. Every question of man's morality, the idea of justice, what it means to be good, everything. I've solved it and you understand that it has been solved. If an Insurrection member performs an action that gives us an advantage, it is therefore a moral action. If it gives us a disadvantage, it is therefore an immoral action. Base everything on the foundation of Advantage and everything falls into place neatly.

"There is no law, only power. There exists no impartiality, only hidden conviction. Victory is all but assured. You can lie, cheat, kill, and steal while honestly condemning your opponents for lying, cheating, killing, and stealing all the while being completely consistent, technically. None of these men can understand this on the deeper levels, but you do. I can tell. You can still recognize when you're lying."

All the cells in Oliver's brain and heart were burning. He didn't have the energy to deal with this right now.

"Just tell me what to do," Oliver said

"Precisely what I told you before. Trade weapons with one of the guys with a rifle, get one with a scope. Shoot on my signal."

"Okay," said Oliver, "What happened in Circle Park on the day of the Slaughtering?"

"You don't know?" Reece said

"I think I do."

"What do you think happened?"

"A group of ten got fed up with the government trying to put their publication out of business for being critical of them. There were frivolous arrests and releases of the staff. Finally all ten of them decided to protest in public, completely ignoring the latest round of crackdowns justified by falsely inflating the danger of terrorist actions. Then they shot them all dead when they refused to disperse."

"Then that's how it happened."

"Is it, though?"

"What do you mean?"

"How do you know?"

"The graves for one. Secondly, it's what kicked this war off. I distinctly remember when it happened and the rage I felt when I was told."

"How do *you* think it happened?"

"Precisely how you described it, Oliver."

Oliver was getting annoyed. All he wanted was confirmation, something solid to hold onto, a piece of information that would outright destroy all of the propaganda that seeped out of The Vigil's press. He hadn't read a word of a Vigil pamphlet in over twenty years. Not even the man who appeared to know almost everything would give him anything to work with.

"How do we prove it to The Vigil? You've heard

their stories. How can we rub it in their faces that they kicked off all of this death?"

"They'll never listen to the truth. They're too far gone. They don't care about what is true and they're only interested in killing all of us. This is why we can't cripple ourselves by caring about it either. Shackling ourselves to the 'truth' reduces our effectiveness. If they gave a damn about that this war would've been over before it started. Now go trade your weapon."

Oliver walked over to the other men and discovered that they had used his journal to keep the fire going.

"You sons of bitches!" Oliver shouted as he quickly moved towards the fire.

"Don't get your panties in a bunch. Nobody even read it," one of the men fired back. The group began laughing at him.

"Reece told me to trade weapons with one of you. Somebody give me a fucking rifle."

The older man stood up, went to the corner of the room, grabbed his rifle and handed it to Oliver. Oliver took the revolver out of his belt and handed it to him. The old man's droopy eyes were stoic and sedative.

Oliver looked toward the floor, "Thanks."

"You're welcome," the old man replied.

They'd destroyed that chance at historical recognition. A first person account of this pivotal stage in the war might've lasted generations. Oliver had nothing else to fall back on. No one remembers librarians and random Insurrection members during a small-scale raid. If anything the book would read: "Reece took a small squad of men to scout out a Vigil warehouse, raid it, and take a negligible amount of food home." His legacy now rested in being the right-hand of Reece, the solider and philosopher. He was alright with that. At least he had to be. Only the best and worst people make History, and Oliver was neither of these. He may never be a household name in History courses for hundreds of years, but at least he was fighting for what was right.

After a meal of stale bread and spongy tinned meat the men began preparing to take the warehouse. The fire was out and everything was dark aside from muddled moonbeams made blurry by clouded and blocked windows.

The men descended the staircase. The clanging of boots on thin metal steps got quieter and quieter. Oliver took the butt of the rifle and tried to break the window through the tiny hole in the boards. He hit it once. Twice. Three times. Nothing. Not even a crack. He would just have to shoot through it.

Through the scope Oliver saw the men creeping up on the outpost. Turning the rifle toward the enemy windows, he saw that the Vigil agents had been drinking. They were passing a bottle around, smiling and laughing. It was a little different seeing their faces. This wasn't just a fantasy anymore. He was about to take another man's life.

He whirled the scope back down to Reece who ordered two of the men to set up crossfire along another corner of the building. It looked like Reece was going to have them shoot through the windows. Reece turned around and looked into Oliver's eye. He pointed to him and mouthed the word, "Now."

Oliver steadied his aim. Which one would he shoot? He chose one heavy-set agent who was leaning back in his chair. He looked like he was in the middle of telling a story, everyone was listening to him intently. Maybe he commanded the men? Oliver hated him and his stupid grin. Sitting on a massive stockpile of rations and letting children of the Insurrection starve. He deserved to die. It was perfectly logical to hate him. Oliver's finger inched onto the trigger, he steadied his aim, and fired.

He missed.

The man fell back in his chair. The window shattered. The Vigil agents frantically ran around searching for their weapons. A couple of men had a sidearm attached to their belts. Oliver didn't shoot a second time.

Windows crashed. Bullets flew. Lots of faint screaming. He saw a couple of last breaths used for whimpering screams. A grenade exploded. The old man he traded weapons with was shot in the shoulder. After the first exchange all but the old man and Reece were dead on the Insurrection side. Only one Vigil agent was left standing. Reece hid. The old man was shot in the middle of the forehead as the last agent carefully searched around. Oliver could see the heat leaving the old man's body in the frosty wind. The mist of life evaporated and blended with the natural gases of the air until there was nothing left but the cold again.

Reece and the last remaining agent played a short game of cat and mouse until finally Reece stabbed him in the neck after a short struggle. The agent tried to reach for his gun as the blood spurted from his neck, but Reece held his hand into the ground while it leaked out of him.

Oliver slung the rifle over his shoulder, descended the stairs and rushed over. All of the faces of the dead were haunting. None of them had their eyes closed. None of them had a straight face or a slight grin. None of them looked like a poorly done make-up job during an open casket funeral. Every face was like their last emotion was frozen in time. Every single expression was panic except for the old man's which looked sad and disappointed.

Oliver's revolver was a few feet away from the body. He picked it up and put it back on his belt. Reece was breathing very heavily. They looked at each other and stepped over the broken windows into the building. Pallets and pallets of non-perishable food were stacked high all around.

"How are we going to carry all of this back?" Oliver asked

"We aren't, think of the logistics of this whole excursion. How many men did we start with? How much food could we reasonably carry in those packs? How many people would that feed? For how long? You're not thinking long-term, Oliver. You're smarter than this."

"Then why the hell did all these men die? What was it for?" Oliver said, holding back anger.

"This is how I'm going to win this war."

"By letting all of your men die."

Reece sighed, widened his eyes, and walked closer to Oliver. He spoke through his teeth as if he'd been personally betrayed by a life-long friend. The rage was pure and perfect.

"I know what I'm talking about, and what I'm doing. You're letting death mess with your critical faculties. Once the shock subsides you'll be able to think clearly again. Advantage. We have it now. Against both Nicholas and the Vigil."

He was right. Oliver wasn't thinking straight.

"I think they have someone in the back. I saw them bringing food back there," Oliver said, dropping the subject.

"Check it out."

Oliver opened the back office. In the corner, behind a shelf, he saw the quivering shape of a child. He had to have been about twelve. His hair was dirty and unkempt. Crooked teeth that were too big for his mouth. The clothes that he had on were far too big for him. He kept one of his hands hidden from view.

"Are you okay?" Oliver asked

He shook his head no and desperately tried to back up further behind the shelf, but only ended up pressing up harder against the back wall.

"Did they hurt you?" Oliver asked again, reaching his hand out and crouching down to meet their eyes.

The kid shook his head no again, and looked even more frightened seeing the scar on Oliver's hand.

"What is your name?" Oliver asked.

The kid murmured something.

"What?"

"Alex!" the kid screamed.

Reece entered the room after hearing the voice and stomped in the direction of the child.

"Show me your hand."

"No!" The kid yelled.

"Show me your goddamned hand!" Reece shouted.

He struggled with the kid's arm for a moment or two until he was able to unearth the sharp "V" tattoo imprinted on the back of his hand.

"I knew it," Reece said, "Shoot him."

"Wait, wait. We can remove the tattoo and bring him back. Might make a decent recruit later on?" Oliver pleaded.

"Nope, after seeing what we did he'll be too resentful. Wouldn't possibly work. We can't trust him. It's the only way."

Everything in Oliver's heart and gut told him not to go through with this, but he could hear Reece's voice in his head already. Telling him how short-sighted he was. How necessary this was, how great men had to make difficult choices, and how he was letting his emotions get the better of him. The argument was playing out in his head already. They accept pride in the Insurrection and hatred of the Vigil as emotions only because they are advantageous to what must be accomplished. Any emotion that gets in the way of the struggle is irrational and a product of latent brainwashing that one had to work themselves out of.

He couldn't get wrapped up in sentimentality now. Oliver drew his revolver and looked down at Alex. The child's eyes looked more terrifying than those of any grown man. They were bright green and filled with terror, wrath and indignation. It was as if Alex knew that he could rip out Oliver's throat with his teeth, but decided against it. It was too late to save him now. Alex already hated him for considering the choice in the first place. Oliver pointed his revolver at the child. The kid would become one of them. It was the most likely outcome. He would don the uniform and jitter with joy as he slaughtered. He'd stand post and place bullets in the skulls of innocent people trying to cross The Divide. He'd take his pocket knife and mark his kill count in the wooden planks that provided his cover in the towers overlooking the border, and then he'd compare his score with his colleagues and the person who took the least amount of life would have to buy the drinks that evening. The ethical thing to do would be to end his life here. Now. Prevent him from being the inevitable murderer his society conditions him to be.

Why hadn't he pulled the trigger yet? Why was he ruminating?

"Let's go," Reece said.

Oliver held the gun between Alex's eyes. He closed his own eyes, fired and rushed out of the room. Despite averting his eyes, the truth was still there concealed behind a thin wall. The murdered boy's eyes were wide open and looking up at the blank grey wall. It might've been the last thing he saw if he had any brief moment of consciousness after the bullet pierced his brain.

Oliver felt dead.

"Help me out with this.." Reece ordered, "I need to get the bodies all piled up in a corner away from the stacks of food."

Oliver never tried to move a dead body before, but they were heavier than any living person. Death has weight. Each one of them felt like they were made of solid lead. Reece set his backpack down, took out a camera, and handed it to Oliver.

"Alright, we have to be quick with this because they might've radioed it in," Reece said.

Oliver aimed the camera at Reece and the large pallet of canned food. Reece took off his jacket and slung it around his shoulder so the Torch of the Insurrection was facing the camera. He leaned his elbow on one of the stacked pallets. Reece narrowed his eyes and looked diagonally as if he was looking into the sun coming up over the horizon. Oliver snapped the photo.

"Good?" Reece said.

"Yeah," Oliver said.

Oliver turned away and looked at the entrance to the back office. His eyes moved to the floor. What had he argued himself into doing? Then he felt a sharp pain against the back of his head. Oliver fell face first onto the floor. His vision was cloudy and his brain was slow due to the impact. His eyes instinctively closed, there was a stabbing pain in the side of his neck and an immense weight pushing down on his back. He struggled for around twenty seconds and then gave up.

He heard Reece's voice as he slipped into non-feeling, "You understand, don't you?"

Then he felt nothing.

PART 2

CHAPTER SIX

THE FIRST THING HE FELT WAS HIS BACK ON A COLD rock-hard surface, then a musty smell, then an intense throbbing pain ravaging the back of his head. For a few moments Oliver kept his eyes closed. He imagined he was back at the library taking a nap and drooling on his desk surrounded by annoyed people, where the worst part of the day was opening a heavy door and dealing with loud bratty ignoramuses who never understood that he didn't control when the pamphlets get delivered.

It was nice for a little while to imagine opening his eyes and revealing the shelves of books he'd kept watch over for so long. He dreamed of reading one after Reece injected him with what must've been a strong sedative. There were no words in them, just a bunch of garbled splotches of ink, but he was enjoying himself immensely. The pain was pulsing inside of his head now, and he ached everywhere. It was time to shove himself back into the real world.

His glasses were gone so every far away edge had

some fuzz and ripple to it. He was in a cell. There were no windows. A small metal cot was on its side and up against the opposite wall. It was a gross metal thing, not much more than some stretched cloth and a bunch of thick tent poles. It was better than the floor at least. A toilet was in the corner complete with functioning plumbing. The ceramic was cracked and scratched, but it appeared to be working. The handle was on a tall hydrant looking metal piece sticking out of the top. The walls were crumbly and worn, but still rather sturdy.

The bars were thin and close to one another. It would be difficult to stick his entire arm out of the cage let alone his head. There was a staircase leading to a large metal door that shut the room in what appeared to be a basement. He struggled from lying on his back to a sitting position with his back against the far wall. He lightly touched the back of his head and wriggled his fingers through his hair searching for the wound. It was tender and swollen. It felt like his head was in the agonizing process of growing a second skull out of the back of his scalp. Oliver pressed on various parts of the injury grunting and clenching his teeth with each gentle bit of pressure. He examined his fingers. No bleeding.

After taking a couple of hard deep breaths he forced himself to his feet and walked over to the bars to get a read on where he was. The hallway looked long enough for around three other cells. Hanging on the ceiling outside of his cell were bright artificial lights emitting a faint buzzing sound. Oliver had to squint his eyes tightly to get a rough estimate of what they looked like. They were shaped like tubes. Taking direction from the pain in his body, he set up the cot and lied down on his stomach. The gravity of the situation started to take hold, and it felt like every single organ he possessed gained fifty pounds. His hands began shaking, his mind projected a reel of possible deaths, and the only thing that would stop the fear from driving him mad was to turn it to anger.

Oliver pounded his fist into the side of the cot, whispering obscenities in rhythm with the punches. For a short moment he hated Reece and each faction of this war with equal vigor, but then stopped himself from continuing that line of emotion. Why should he stop? What's the point? He was in prison there's no need to put on any kind of face.

Part of him was thankful to be in prison. Now he could rest. Oddly enough, he felt somewhat free. There's no word for that feeling that covered him then like a steel cloak. It's too strong for a word. It's a feeling that hits harder than love. That distinct sickly combination of self-pity and reluctant acceptance that comes with knowing the fact that the world is falling to pieces directly in front of you, and there is nothing you can do about it. He thought of Edward then. He didn't want to tell him any of these stories anymore. The poor guy wouldn't be able to handle it.

No, this was one of the moments that tests how strong one's loyalty is. Oliver tried to fight off all of his negative thoughts, feelings, and intuitions about Reece and the Insurrection. Certainly he had a good reason for doing what he did. Some of the feelings of betrayal stayed, but he attempted to funnel those emotions into general despair about his present circumstances. It didn't completely work. There was no possible way that Reece knew they wouldn't kill him on the spot. Why was he alive anyway? What were they keeping him for?

He flipped over and stared at the spackled uneven

ceiling. He imagined the green farming town again. He was running around outside of a barn and his parents were watching him through the second story window holding each other. It was a time when nothing hurt, no one died, everyone was reasonable, everything good lasted forever, everything bad no longer existed, and the world was free and happy. What he wouldn't give for that relief of being cooled off during a warm day by a brisk breeze.

It was all fighting now though. Half of the world hurt, half of the world would die, half of the world would starve, half was reasonable, everything good was trodden upon, everything bad was exalted and praised, and half of the world was tyrannized by the other half. He was nostalgic for a past that never happened and dreading a future that already came into being. Oliver walked toward the cell bars and started yelling for the guards. He hoped he could extract some rudimentary information about where he was from a hostile conversation.

"Hello?" Oliver yelled, "Hello, I need help!"

"They won't be able to hear you," a voice responded. It was coming from the cell next to him.

"Who are you?" Oliver said.

"They sound-proof the rooms because the leadership thinks the Insurrection will corrupt their minds. They're very frightened of you people."

"Okay, who are you?" Oliver asked.

"I'm Thomas. Also, they force the guards to wear noise-cancelling headphones when they deliver the food every day when one of your kind is imprisoned here. I have to stop myself from laughing every time I see them come down here in their big tough uniforms with those ridiculous earmuffs on. Not like they can hear me on the other side anyway when they leave."

"Are you Vigil or Insurrection?"

"Will you believe me?"

"I don't know. Depends."

"It's not like I can physically show you my hand from here, can I?"

"Just tell me then"

"Every single person who gets thrown down here is all about the 'which colors do you fly' horseshit. Could you be a little different please?"

"You're stalling. You're Vigil aren't you?"

"I'm in one of their prisons you know?"

"So? You could just be a common criminal that still believes in the cause."

"Would you believe me if I said I didn't believe in the cause?"

"Probably not. I wasn't born yesterday."

"Sure sounds like you were."

"Whatever, I'm not talking to you anymore."

"Suit yourself."

They were silent for a couple of hours. Oliver sat on his cot facing the opposite wall trying to keep his mind occupied. Thomas shuffled around a bit in his cell.

"So let's say I were Vigil, right? What's the harm in talking to me?" Thomas asked.

"There's no point. All you're going to try and do is persuade me to stop fighting for the Insurrection. And you'll say anything and lie about anything in order to do so. No thank you. Not interested."

"But you have that same opportunity with me, don't you? You could lie to me and try to get me to join the Insurrection. You could corrupt me until I'm the most vigorous supporter you've ever had. Least we can do is talk. Sitting here in silence for so long turns a man crazy, most of you don't last long."

"They kill us?"

"I don't know, probably. Generally you show up, they give you just enough food to stay alive, then after a month or two they take you out of those doors up the stairs and you don't come back. Can't say if they die for sure, but most likely."

Oliver's muscles stiffened, "No..."

"Look, it wouldn't do me much good to recruit you if I am Vigil because you'd die before you'd be of any use to me. They like to torture through starvation too so I'll make you a deal. They treat me pretty well around here. I've been here a long time. They feed me decent meals, and so far they haven't taken me away. So, I'll give you some of my rations every day if you'll just keep talking to me. We have a deal?"

"I'll think about it."

"That's the best answer I've gotten so far. Let me know."

"Alright then."

They were silent for another couple of minutes.

Thomas piped up again, "We don't even have to talk about the war or politics or philosophy or anything like that if you don't want."

"I *said* I will think about it. I'm a bit preoccupied with my death sentence right now."

"Okay, sorry. I mean I don't know what happens it's just an assumption really."

"Stop, that's enough."

Oliver slumped over and cupped his face in his hands. He squeezed his eyes shut and inhaled deeply. What a terrible and meaningless end. He didn't want to break the silence with sobbing, and so he cried as quietly as his body would let him. Edward would never know for sure what happened to him. What would they say? The only rational explanation was to either slap him on a list of political martyrs, or pretend like he died during the raid. They couldn't forget about him completely because Reece had that picture and people would ask questions about who took it, right? On some level, they'd be happy for his present circumstances as it gives them another grievance to hold up against the Vigil. The whole situation would be nothing more than a footnote in a speech, an additional talking point added to the section that listed all of the horrors perpetrated by the enemy.

For a few years it seemed like everyone was dripping madness and couldn't find a solid grip anywhere. Politicians were exclaiming proudly what one would expect to hear from a crazed drug fiend that was a few hours late to his next fix. People were either terrified or just as insane as their chosen political conduit. It was unexplainable to every historian, psychologist, statistician, or any expert for that matter. *The Philosophy of Advantage* relaxed everyone at a time when they desperately needed a mental sedative. It destroyed all uncertainty, it shattered every higher principle man had ever held dear, and it soothed every case of cognitive dissonance that one might experience in any kind of struggle for power for even if something appears to be hypocritical, the reasoning behind the acts was perfectly intellectually consistent.

What it didn't offer though was a field guide on how to survive prison. Its only advice in these situations was to either accept death if you couldn't handle torture, or if you could, do everything in your power to inconvenience your tormentors before accepting it.

Oliver was going to miss this week's pamphlet, and he was getting antsy. Not only was he to die, but he wasn't even allowed to distract himself from the thought.

He heard a loud clanking sound coming from the top of the staircase. This was not the kind of distraction he was hoping for. Oliver shot up and scrambled to the far corner of the prison cell. He huddled there with his back against the wall and pressing himself harder and harder against it with every crack of the boots against the stone. He clenched his fists together, there was only one of them. He looked like a man who'd grown up on a planet with twice Earth's gravitational pull. Short legs, short arms, massive core and a square-shaped head. He was swimming inside of his helmet, and he was wearing enormous headphones. He was carrying a tray atop which was a modest nutritional meal of grilled chicken, four toasted slices of bread, two boiled potatoes, and two raw carrots. The man took great pains to avoid looking in Oliver's direction. The guard moseyed over to Thomas' cell.

Oliver rushed to the front of his cell, pressing his face against the bars trying to get a decent look. The guard gently placed the tray on the floor and then unsheathed his pistol. With the other hand he grabbed a set of keys, unlocked the door, opened it, and then slid the tray into the cell with his foot. Oliver heard the cell door slam, and the guard struggled back up the stairs slamming the door behind him as he left and the loud smashing of metal on stone hung in the stale air for a brief moment, reverberating off of the naked skeletal walls.

Thomas exploded with laughter.

"Gets me every single time! It was like they put a

watermelon on top of a milk crate that guy. Did you see him? Waddling like a penguin that just shit itself."

Oliver said nothing. Thomas' low rumbling chuckle went on for another few seconds and then subsided. Sleep called to him again, but he was worried about the age old warning concerning post-concussion rest. Maybe he could fade away slowly in his dreams and keep the satisfaction of ending his life from the Vigil. Oliver closed his eyes for a few minutes, turned onto his side, and tried to reinvigorate his imagination into bringing him back to the apartment with Edward. He could put forms together, sounds, smells, but it was nothing like the first time he woke up. The memory of where he actually was held firm inside of that long welt that still pulsed with pain during every heartbeat, distorting the color and picture of the daydream with each short punch of agony like someone was rhythmically slapping the top of an old television.

Thomas was still chewing his food violently and it echoed in the hallway. There was no way Oliver was getting to sleep during one of his meals. He sighed heavily, turned onto his other side and faced the wall directly. He focused on the minute patterns inside of the chipped stone wall and they began to wiggle and wave, and he studied the optical illusion for around fifteen minutes. A small skittering noise rang out. Oliver sat up and saw two slices of toasted bread and a carrot sitting outside of his cell on the floor. The carrot rolled a little bit. He rose from the cot and walked over to the bars.

"Hey," Thomas said, "I tossed a couple..."

"Yeah I see them. Just have to stretch a bit."

Oliver went prone and stuck his arm sideways through the thin gaps. He was able to reach the food and drag it into his cell with a bit of straining. Oliver dusted them off with his clothing and ate them happily. He didn't realize how hungry he was until the first bite. It was just enough to keep him satisfied for now.

"I never actually..." Oliver said

"I know."

CHAPTER SEVEN

Four sleep-cycles went by before Oliver spoke to Thomas again. There was no way to tell when day or night was in that tiny windowless prison. The lights never went out and their constant humming was no help when trying to comfortably drift off. They hadn't fed him yet, but Oliver had been grifting off of Thomas' meals every day in order to survive. Unwittingly, he had trained himself to wait by the bars of the cell towards the end of Thomas' loud savage demolishing of the wide variety of courses that were brought to him once a day. The day before last they'd brought him a few skirt steaks complete with grilled asparagus and whipped garlic potatoes. Thomas threw him the asparagus and Oliver remembered fuming over not being given any meat, but he kept his mouth shut out of fear that his prison mate's generosity would relax if he got too uppity. On this day they brought Thomas a large bowl of rustic soup. Judging by the smell it was chicken with some kind of wild rice and mushroom, and the room was filled with a joyous chorus of slurping and chewing.

Oliver spoke up, "I'm guessing because..."

Thomas guzzled his way through the last of the soup, "Yep, can't exactly throw soup. Normally they give me a couple pieces of toast to go along with it."

Oliver felt a bubble of air gurgle out of his stomach and into his throat. He tried to force it out of his esophagus in the hope that it would ease the hunger pains a bit, but it retreated back down his gullet before much could be done about it.

"So, Thomas how old are you?"

"Very."

"How long have you been in here?"

"A long time."

"I thought you wanted to talk to me?"

"Do you actually want to know this stuff?"

"Yes, I do."

"When I was thrown in here I was so frightened that I forgot to keep track of the days at first. Every Sunday they bring one of their pamphlets to me so I've been logging the time that way. I'm seventy-eight. Been in this cell for thirty-one years."

"Dear God..."

"Do you believe in God?"

"No, just an expression."

It was silent for a few moments.

"Maybe that was too strong a question. I apologize." Thomas said.

Oliver reassured him, "No, no it's okay. Legitimate question."

"I've always wanted to ask someone, if humanity were its own God, would it be more Old Testament or New? This prison is like my own personal bunker. Both for my head and body, but the only downside is that I have no one to discuss anything with."

"You speak of humanity as if you aren't a part of it."

"In a sense I'm not. The world out there has been overtaken by war. I've been in here for the entirety of it. People are different. I'm not much of a person anymore, more like an antique nightstand or an old radio."

"Do *you* believe in God?" Oliver asked.

"No, it's just interesting to think about."

No one spoke for another few moments.

"Why are you in here?" Thomas asked.

"I got captured during a raid on a Vigil storehouse. The Insurrection was running low on food stocks so we were ordered to steal some."

"That's...interesting," Thomas said with an undertone of disbelief

"Why? Seems pretty simple to me. Low on food, you go get some."

"Pamphlet delivered here two weeks ago said that you folks were enjoying a surplus, and your cutting off of Vigil supply lines were causing *them* to starve."

"You can't trust that garbage. They're always pumping out propaganda trying to make us look evil."

"So, you did not have a surplus then? And the Vigil was not low on supplies?"

"Absolutely not! Think about it. Did they ever stop bringing your meals? Did you ever actually go without food? Did they ever issue cutbacks to try and stretch their dwindling supply?"

"Those are decent points. Did any of that happen to you?"

Oliver paused for a moment. He was never lacking food. There was no cutback on rations announced, nothing of the sort. He had the opportunity to convert Thomas now.

Oliver lied, "Yes."

"I don't believe you."

"What? Why not?"

Thomas raised his voice, "Because it's in your interest to say that, isn't it? It's always the same with you types. You have absolutely no idea what it's like trying to think about the here and now when you have no access to the truth and everyone is trying to make stupid legalistic cases for everything. You have all of the truth right in front of you and you spit on it. Ridiculously stupid."

"Stupid? It's not like there's any way for you to know better!"

Oliver closed his eyes and sighed heavily. Immediately he knew that he had said the wrong thing, that he'd let the true content of his mind lay naked in front of someone who was possibly the enemy. He'd committed a fundamental mistake.

"Exactly," Thomas said after a few minutes of revealing stillness, "Even in prison, with the knowledge of your soon-coming death, you *still* try to recruit people. If you're not going to be honest with me, don't bother speaking. This isn't the only prison you're in my friend. You give me one story, they give me another."

Another couple of hours went by as Oliver wallowed in a combination of guilt and frustration. Thomas' fried voice piped up again, "I should be angry with you for lying to me. But I just don't have the energy anymore. I'm an old man. Over the years I've watched my hands grow wrinkled and bony. Every morning it's a struggle to get out of bed. If I exert any of my dwindling energy on useless things like anger I might not make it until the next day."

"Alright, look I'm sorry" Oliver said.

"It's okay, war makes a madman out of everyone. Can I tell you a quick story?"

"Alright, shoot."

"It took place in Kansas, or what would soon be Kansas, back in the mid-1800s. There were two brothers named Cody and William Powell. Their father was the owner of a large fortune attained through a lifetime of shrewd business. Legal, but shrewd. Both of them resented their father for amassing that wealth in the cold and callous way he had, so they resolved to take just enough for both of them to move out West and start a simpler life for themselves and the rest they would use to hire people to build almshouses in the towns they'd stopped in along their trip. One day they stop in a relatively boring town. Nothing interesting ever happened in this small backwater place, they'd be lucky if they saw a tumbleweed roll by. Anyhow, the Powells introduce themselves and stay there for a few days, and by this time they'd told everyone their story. The townspeople hatch a plan in order to cure their terminal case of boredom. They send two groups of people out to meet with each brother alone during their daily routines, and convince them that the other is secretly planning on killing them and taking the rest of dad's fortune for himself."

"Initially, neither believed it. They laughed it off as ridiculous. But as the days rolled by little innocuous things began being seen as evidence of foul play. Cody stays out slightly longer than usual one day, so William then decides to check in with the bank to make sure all the money is there every day, and then Cody gets suspicious of his brother visiting the bank. Quietly, they both became paranoid of the other until one afternoon when they were both getting a drink, Cody made a sudden movement toward his waistband and William, being the faster shot and thinking Cody was finally going to try to murder him, killed his brother right there in the bar in front of everyone. The townspeople had been staring the whole time waiting for something to happen. William broke down in tears when he saw that Cody only had a coin in his hand. He was reaching into his pocket to pay the bartender. The sheriff was summoned, arrested William, and sentenced him to hanging. William was executed in front of all of the lying townspeople, they all remarked about how it was a damn shame, and then continued to lead their lives as if nothing had happened."

Oliver was sitting down with his back nuzzled up against the wall adjacent to Thomas' cell, and he was clutching his knees like he was a schoolchild again hiding in a closet during a game of hide-and-seek.

"Did that really happen?" Oliver asked.

"No idea, but I like the story," Thomas replied.

"Me too."

"Whose fault do you think it is?"

"What?"

"Who do you think is responsible for what happened?"

"I don't really know, but all of it started with the lying townspeople. I'd say them if I had to answer."

"That's what most people say. Not that it's a bad answer, but everyone forgets about the brothers allowing themselves to be manipulated like that. There was a lack of trust there. They believed the word of complete strangers over their own sibling. Could've stopped all of it by talking to each other about what the townspeople said to them. Instead they let it fester and distanced themselves from one another."

"Never thought of it that way. I suppose everyone is a little bit guilty."

Thomas quietly laughed and wheezed, "Yeah, they are."

"Old," Oliver said.

"Hey, come on now!" Thomas replied.

"No, not you. Old Testament. I never answered that question. Definitely Old, at least now. Very violent, temperamental, callous, unforgiving. At least that's what I've heard about what the Bible says. Never read it."

"When I was out there, I noticed that people believed in the type of God they needed. Very well-adjusted and kind-mannered people believed in a God that was heavy-handed when exacting justice. A kind of 'smite the evil' business. Those who were very unstable, criminal elements, or people that made lots of mistakes in life lean toward a forgiving God. One that will absolve you of your sins if you truly feel remorse about it. They each want a God that can do what they could never do themselves."

"I'm not really knowledgeable about this stuff."

"Same here, it's just an observation. I'm no missionary."

"Where did you hear that story?"

"Oh, I must have read it somewhere at some point. Can't remember where. Do you have any stories for me?"

"No, I can't remember the last time I read a book and I worked in a library believe it or not."

"That's a shame."

Oliver felt a dart of shame as the word left Thomas' lips. All that time and all those resources squandered. The preoccupation with Victory was important though. No one is willing to expose themselves with an act that might deescalate for fear of being vulnerable to attacks from the enemy.

"Actually, I do have a story," Oliver said quietly

"Hit me," Thomas said with child-like eagerness

"A Vigil journalist, in an attempt to smear the Insurrection, covered his tattoo with flesh-colored make-up and hired an artist to recreate a pinkish scar in its place to blend in. He'd spent three months in Insurrection territory interviewing and investigating. He'd finally mangled enough quotes and gathered enough out of context information together to craft a decent investigative propaganda piece. He left that night and snuck himself all the way back to the Divide. When he was just out of sight he poured some alcohol on his hand, trying to wash away the fake scar. Unfortunately, the artist had made the scar nearly permanent due his insistence on accuracy and durability. He ran up to the Divide and began waving his arms frantically, explaining that he was a Vigil journalist and he has an amazing story that he wants to publish in order to undermine the work of the Insurrection. None of the Vigil agents standing post believed him, and so they shot him dead in the cold."

"I could see it happening." Thomas said.

"It did." Oliver replied.

Thomas didn't respond.

"Do you think the war will ever end?" Oliver asked.

"No," Thomas said after a few moments of silence.

"Why not?"

"I've lost hope in trying. Before everything started

spiraling I tried to convince people that war was not the correct course of action. That other things could be done. Nobody wanted to listen to me. All too caught up."

"You can't be forgetting about Circle Park though."

"Only heard about it through the papers back then. You couldn't trust any of them, even then, and I wasn't there to see it myself. I was locked up shortly after that incident. People started treating it like it was the only moment in history that mattered. You'd think history began with Circle Park the way they wrote about it. As if those gunshots exploded the Universe into being."

"Who do you think was at fault *there*?" Oliver asked in a smug tone.

"I don't know, since I wasn't there." Thomas said.

"Just piece it together from what you've read. I saw it happen as a child."

"I don't know, since I wasn't there. And did you really?" Thomas repeated slower.

"I'm pretty sure I did. Don't you care about what started all of this? The intricate details of that day?"

"Of course I do, but I'll never get them because I wasn't there. At this point it really doesn't matter who started it."

"Insurrection pamphlets have written about this for years now. There were ten people that were finally fed up with the..."

"Yeah, yeah save it."

"What?"

"I don't know which story to trust and so I'd rather believe nothing about it. Knowing this won't change anything."

"How can you possibly believe nothing about one of the most important events in History?"

"I'm doing it as we speak."

"You're *actually* giving Vigil propaganda weight?"

"I'm giving their propaganda the same credence I give yours. They claim that they had to shoot armed terrorists threatening to storm a government office, your guys killed a few of them, and the Vigil agents are buried there."

"Ridiculous," Oliver said dismissively, "It's no wonder you don't believe in doing anything, you can't even get past the first stage of selecting a truth."

"Selecting a truth?" Thomas asked.

"*The Philosophy of Advantage* states that one must believe things on the basis of whether or not it provides an Advantage. So the Insurrection can never be accused of lying due to the fact that we honestly believe what we are saying. Even if we don't actually believe what we are saying, we only lie so as to provide an Advantage to the Insurrection either in narrative formation or military strategy. The practice of lying within the ranks of the Insurrection is either moot because lying assumes the speaker secretly doesn't believe his own words, or the act is excusable for the direct result of trying to win the war against the Vigil, thus preventing evil. Who in their right mind *wouldn't* lie if it meant they could prevent evil befalling their fellow man?

"You look at the different interpretations of an event, or competing narratives, and you weigh the pros and cons. How will I be perceived by others if I believe this? Does honestly believing this provide me with an argumentative Advantage? Will believing this provide me with the motivation I need to continue fighting The Vigil? Then whatever you select *is* the truth in that moment, everyone *must* choose the same general assortment of facts or else we're implicitly accusing those on our side of being ignorant or liars and this infighting only gives the Vigil an opening to strike us, both mentally and physically. You have to believe things to both maintain intellectual consistency and a good view in the public eye, even if you don't believe it, you have to make yourself honestly believe it."

"I learned that the truth is what *is*."

"That is an outdated tautology. No one is interested in that version of truth anymore. It didn't persuade anyone, and so in the midst of the war we needed to adapt."

"Who are you persuading now? The Vigil has adopted this outlook as well."

"You, I suppose. I don't fault them for lying. I fault them for lying to further evil ends. Do you generally root for *either* side?"

"I don't root. Is there truly only one man in the country that doesn't?"

"If there are others I haven't seen them."

"And you only lie to further the good?"

"Correct"

"What is *the good*?"

"Victory over the Vigil."

No one said anything for a moment. Thomas sighed and then spoke solemnly.

"I just want to sit here. Eat my dinners. Read my pamphlet every Sunday. Laugh at how ridiculous the guards look. And remember when I used to hope that one day somebody would walk through that metal door over there wearing a t-shirt and jeans and tell me that the war is over, and it doesn't matter what the hell is on my hand anymore. I sat here for over thirty years hoping every single day that it would happen, and it hasn't. It won't happen for me. "

"The Insurrection might end it and free you?"

"You don't understand."

"What?"

"It will still matter what is on my hand no matter the outcome. There is no Victory condition for someone like me. For you, maybe. But me, no. There's no Advantageous choice for me here. The Vigil will think I'm being deceptive if I choose to join their cause after such a long resistance, and they'll kill me if I choose to join yours. It's nothing but daily loss and I've made a painful peace with that. I will enjoy laughing and eating in here, by myself, and be comforted by the fact that I'm not contributing to this travesty."

"Not like you're doing anything to fix it either. At least I'm making the attempt."

"I've made attempts of my own," Thomas lowered his voice, "They say some of the worst atrocities are the result of good intentions."

"I'm sure they are, and 'no positive results' is always the result of non-action."

"There's nothing I could possibly do at this stage to help make things better, which is why I've chosen what I've chosen."

"Fine," Oliver said, "but you'll have to live with that."

"So will you. At least you're speaking honestly now."

"You know, I don't really care what's on your hand. If I'm going to be forced into honesty you should be too. What is on it?"

"Nothing."

"What do you mean nothing?"

"Exactly that. The reigning government made it mandatory for everyone to get this stamp of loyalty put onto their hands to avoid radicalization and remind themselves daily of 'whose side they were on.' A stupid request for a single person let alone a whole nation. I told my wife for years that it was because I wasn't going to put up with this overbearing abuse of power, but the reality is I was just afraid of needles. Ever since I was a child I couldn't deal with them. I've never admitted this to anyone before. I had a stencil cut perfectly to the dimensions of the *V* tattoo, and I drew it on the back of my hand every morning for years. One day I went swimming with my family in one of the public pools, and I'd completely forgotten about it. I was drying myself off and some of it was wiped away. Someone noticed and alerted the authorities. I tried to run, but was stopped by the bystanders. They mobbed me and shoved me up against a chain-link fence holding me in place. A couple of the larger men in the group punched me in the face and stomach a few times. Three men in uniform arrived and threw me in the back of a paddy wagon."

Thomas' voice began to shake, "Last thing I heard before the door closed was my wife screaming, 'How could you do this to us?' The trial wasn't much. The crime was not having a tattoo, not outwardly displaying my loyalty at all times, and quite clearly I was guilty. So they tossed me in here. That's the end of it. No good-byes. I couldn't explain myself. No one would accept any explanation. So pardon me, but fuck you, and fuck your 'struggle.' The last bit of hope I had shot off the Earth when my family sided with the war instead of me. My hand is bare and I intend to keep it that way until I die."

Every word Thomas spoke sounded like it had been clawing out of a deep murky pit infested with the most deadly of beasts for decades and just now reached the surface. Every syllable was tired and worn out, stumbling forward with a limp and collapsing onto the ground, whimpering with joyous relief and unbearable pain like a woman after giving birth. Oliver remembered his own family then. How he left them behind. What would they be saying to him now? If he ever met them again, somehow, would there be any chance of getting them to understand?

"Please," Oliver said softly, "tell me another story."

CHAPTER EIGHT

Every morning the hunger ravenously assaulted Oliver's mind and body, but this morning was particularly brutal. The inadequate sleeping arrangement was contorting the muscles in his back as well. If he turned in the wrong direction too swiftly his torso might detach from its bearings like a defective bottle-cap and crash with a faint splat to the concrete floor, then he'd have to drag his abdomen across the room for a few bread crumbs.

"Hey," Oliver said, "Think you could give me a bit extra today?"

"Sorry," Thomas replied, "No can do."

Oliver pressed his back up against the wall, "Why not?"

"You're more convincing as a starving person if you're actually starving a little bit, and they've been withholding food from you for a while now. If you don't start showing symptoms soon I'm screwed too."

"You've got to be kidding me. I can act like I'm in pain just fine."

"I'm not willing to take that risk, I'm sorry. I won't let it get too bad."

"It's pretty bad now. Feels like a black hole has opened in my stomach."

"This will probably be the worst of it."

"How do you know?"

"Eh, I don't really. I'm just trying to make you feel better."

Oliver chuckled, "Screw you"

Thomas laughed too, "Can you blame me? I have to sit here and listen to the constant moaning."

"I guess not. I haven't been this hungry since I was fifteen."

"What happened then?"

Oliver sat up and leaned forward in his cot, "It was when I first joined up. I had to eat out of garbage cans for a couple days when I was trying to make my way to Circle Park."

"You joined a war at fifteen?"

"It wasn't too much of a war then. People were still reminiscing about times they chucked bricks through Vigil administrative buildings. I was never prepared for what would follow."

"People rarely are."

"I made one crucial mistake though. My father had just finished screaming at me for my insubordination during classes. I'd ball up my exam papers and chuck them to the floor. I'd then rest my head on the desk and pretend my teacher didn't exist. My parents had both gone out, and in a rage I made the choice. I took up the sharpest knife in the kitchen, chomped down on my leather belt, and carved the tattoo off into the sink. I wrapped my hand up with paper towels and scotch tape. I didn't bother cleaning the mess I made."

"How did you think *that* would end?"

"I never really knew. I wasn't thinking that far ahead. I knew the system was stifling me and I hated living under it, so I took a chance on an emerging system. It was amazing while it was happening. The comradery, the joy, the hope. Everyone had fire in their eyes and wanted the same things. After years upon years of feeling alone it was like I'd finally found where I belonged. An opening to a better life and world was emerging and I wanted to be a part of it. Make a mark of some type. Matter, I guess. We all got together and eventually our collective yearning for something new, just and good exploded outward."

The green farming town presented itself again. There was no scar on his hand anymore. He was sitting in a rocking chair on his back porch with a glass of iced whiskey. His children were running around with the family dog on the grass as the sun set behind the mountains. *"Hey, time to come inside kids!"* A woman's voice said from the second story window. The older child asked, *"Come on, Mom please can we play for a few more minutes!"* Oliver then spoke up, *"Oh, I don't know how much harm a few more minutes could do."* The woman's voice then sighed, *"Alright, but not too late okay?"* The children cheered and the dog wagged its tail as the last bit of the reddening sun dipped below the peaks. As the sky darkened Vigil soldiers appeared marching in rhythm over the horizon and covered the foliage with a dark parasitic death that wilted every breath of life.

"Does it still feel that way?"

"Sad thing is, your question made me think of romance for the first time in decades. I can tap into the feeling when I need it I guess. It's an ideal to aspire to, but an ideal without pragmatism is not much more than daydreaming."

"Yeah, but pragmatism without an ideal is self-interested savagery."

"I suppose."

The metal door at the top of the stairs slammed into the wall, and three men started descending. Two of the men were hulking creatures that might as well have had no facial features at all. Everything about them was deadpan and blank aside from a vague resentment that radiated from their minimally furrowed brows, and the muscles flaring in their jowls from gritting teeth. They both stood in front of Oliver's cell and stared inside. Oliver stumbled over to the opposite corner of his cage as Thomas got his meal and Sunday pamphlet delivered to him. There was no laughing this time.

"No! Not today! Not today! No! Not today!" These are the only two things that Oliver could think to say at this point in time. He started saying it with a whisper as soon as he saw the burly men come down the stairs. He started screaming it right into their faces as they opened the doors and grabbed him by the insides of his elbows, one man on each side.

"Not today! No!" Oliver shouted as he struggled, but there was no way his body, malnourished as it was, could put up much of a fight. He tried biting one of the men and got a fist to the stomach for his trouble. Oliver doubled over in pain and a black cloth bag was placed over his head.

"At least let me see! At least let me see!" Oliver screamed, but they couldn't hear him. The short stubby man who delivered the food routed over to Oliver's cell behind him and shoved him forward. The men began to drag Oliver up the stairs, the tops of his feet scraping against the concrete steps.

"Oliver," Thomas said calmly.

"I can't see anything! It's all black, they'll kill me," Oliver said while squirming.

"Don't spend your last moments afraid," Thomas said.

Oliver quieted down as the door crashed shut behind him. The floor turned from concrete to a soft rug which felt like pure bliss for a brief moment, and then to a cold smooth tile-like surface. They must have been walking down a long hallway because no turns were made in a while. As he was being dragged down the hallway the short man behind him would, at random intervals, kick the back of his knees and wheeze with a crackly smoker's laugh, "piece of shit" he would say as he buckled Oliver's legs again and again. Every word the guard said sounded like the linguistic version of dirty street slush. A vile mixture of asphalt, tire rubber, dirt, gravel, and dog piss. If the bag slipped off Oliver expected to see this disgusting concoction dribbling out of his mouth like a poorly-held vomit that left a trail all the way to the prison's entrance.

"Stupid fuck," the guard said as he kicked the back of his legs even harder. Oliver collapsed to the floor onto his knees which send a pang of electric pain up his thighs and down his shins. The two large men held Oliver in place as the third man grumbled, "put this on," and covered him with what felt like the familiar burlap scratchiness of an Insurrection uniform jacket.

"Give it a good beating, make sure to get the head," the short guard ordered.

Oliver was thrown to the ground and mercilessly kicked in the stomach and legs for about a minute. One of the guards pulled the bag off of his head and grabbed him by the hair. There was no time to get a look around before his forehead was whipped into the floor. His vision became blurry, he saw a few sources of fuzzy light and then had the bag shoved back over his head. Oliver tried to say something, but all that came out was a confused and slurred, "Mmmnuh." For a moment he forgot where he was. As they exited the building basic information began to come back to him and the fear crept up again. The fear was the worst part. He missed the dumb concussed state already. A door closed and the chilled wind hit his body. He heard rumblings and chanting in the distance. It got louder and louder as they strolled closer. It was difficult to tell whether the siren of human screeching was angry or excited. Human beings sound exactly the same when they're anticipating a lynching or headline act.

Oliver mentally leafed through *The Philosophy of Advantage* and he'd followed it down to the last punctuation mark, yet this was the fate it carved out for him. That child would've been filled with resentment and exacted revenge on the Insurrection. He may have called for help. That wounded man would've slowed him down and they would've lost two men as opposed to one, and having the numbers was paramount during that raid. Everything he had done was done to give the Insurrection a better foot hold in the fight. Everything sounded reasonable enough, it was all perfectly logical and consistent, but he still felt an immense weight in his chest. He didn't truly believe this. He shot Alex because he was frightened of Reece and could not out-argue him. He condemned that wounded man to death because he, himself, feared death.

He went limp and began silently weeping as the guards dragged him along the sidewalk. The expression-less Vigil agents had to grip his elbows tighter in response, but worrying about pain and bruising was useless now. Even before all of this started happening people spoke as if they were in the middle of a life-and-death political fight. But they were just talking and screaming. Talking and screaming is fine, cathartic almost. Every slight, every small deviation, every pinprick of detachment from the ongoing disagree-ments were rhetorically treated like acts of war until eventually they were treated as such physically. They'd forgotten that they were dealing with other humans.

Oliver's stomach lurched as if the time had finally come to vomit up all of the bad blood. This was it. He killed an innocent person. Although the executioners would just as easily have made the choice that he made in those same circumstances, Oliver felt he deserved Justice. He deserved what was happening to him.

A few hard objects pelted him in the shoulder and head as he was ushered around the corner. It sounded like Vigil members were lined up on the sidewalk jeering and shouting at him. Gallons of venomous spittle flew like grapeshot out of the mouths of these ravenous and vengeful souls, and Oliver felt its acidic heat as it spurted in his direction. They'd become so twisted and so devoid of humanity, or so full of it, that only a cruel death could possibly bring a smile to their lips and calm them down. People have an innate need to vanquish evil and protect good. One hears numerous stories of crowds manufacturing evil so that they may slay it, and pretending that the evil are virtuous so that they may protect them. It's as necessary as eating and sleeping. One was bound to go mad if they didn't routinely satisfy these permanent human urges even at the expense of what they believe, deep in their cores, to be right.

He had finally reached a stage. A few steps. One. Two. Three. Cold on bare feet. Oliver closed his eyes despite already being blinded by the cloth bag. Green farming town. Children. Wife. Edward. Happy Dog. Sunset. Cool Breeze. Warm Air. Hope. Drive. Peace. Life. Freedom. Innovation. Love. He wanted these to be his last visions and feelings. He was ready to go.

Forget where you are now. Be somewhere worth something.

Just then a terrifying wave of cheers exploded from the mouths of the crowd standing beneath him. Oliver's legs were shaking, his shoulders hunched over, scrawny and weak, accepting.

"Thank you. Thank you everyone," a very generic smooth voice said into a microphone, "As all of you know, the elections are underway and my opponents certainly haven't been making it easy on me."

The audience booed.

"Now, now. Respect folks. At the end of the day we're all on the same side here. I am looking forward to serving the Vigil for another term and seeing through the destruction of people like our friend here."

The boos morphed into a more intense scorn.

"He's not our friend! He supports people that kill children," Oliver heard one woman near the front shout.

"You need a candidate that can prove he can withstand the treasonous fraudulent propaganda coming out of the Insurrection. It's tough to figure out what's going on as it is, but types like these, they try to make it even harder for good hard-working people like you to know the truth! And we all know, the truth is what is right and..."

The crowd finished his sentence, "And the Vigil *is* right!"

"Please allow me to ask our friend a question. Sir, who were the Circle Park Ten?"

Oliver didn't answer. One of the guards punched him in the kidney. Oliver doubled over and fell to his knees.

"They got their publication shut down due to government overreach brought on by a crackdown on radicalization. They demonstrated peacefully and were gunned down."

The throng of people started laughing and ridiculing him. The smooth voice behind the microphone started chuckling to himself.

"Sir, were you aware that these 'Circle Park Ten' that you and your kind idolize so much were waving firearms in the faces of innocent people during these demonstrations? One of them even had a bomb strapped to them; there was no other choice for law enforcement. They had to be stopped before they hurt someone."

"Yeah, you moron," someone screamed and threw a rock that hit Oliver in the arm. He was glad he couldn't see their faces in this moment. Their expressions would look all too familiar to him. Teeth bared, tears of joy and rage dripping from opposite eyes, the face of someone who hasn't a care in the world what they're doing and will do practically anything if ordered to.

"You see? This is what happens when you let yourself get taken in by propaganda. You start to believe that up is down, left is right, and what's false is true. Sir, what evidence do you have that can prove that they demonstrated peacefully?"

Oliver had nothing but his memory of the gunshots, "I heard the gunshots as a young boy."

"Did you hear that everyone? He *heard the gunshots*. Isn't that marvelous?"

The crowd hissed and cried out in anger. A few laughed at him. Everybody acted predictably as a crowd would. They cheered and booed and hissed and were quiet when prompted. Nothing is more horrifying, dangerous, and easily controlled than a crowd of politically minded people. Put one of those in the wrong hands, even for the right reasons, and the apocalypse is all but inevitable.

"Just because you *heard* gunshots doesn't necessitate that they came from Vigil weapons."

"You *just* said that Vigil agents shot the 'Circle Park Ten'" Oliver shot back. He realized his mistake instantly.

"Oh look at that. He thinks he has me on the ropes," the voice said with vitriol, "I said that they had to be stopped. That does not necessitate that we did stop them. Unfortunately, our police force's restraint was their downfall and they allowed themselves to be mowed down by your violent band of terrorists. We buried our dead in Circle Park as the Insurrection regrouped, and then when you took over the territory, you took over the narrative too. We thought it would be a moment of peace, but the Insurrection's bloodlust continued long after the event. A woman named 'Danielle' is in the crowd today. Her daughter was slaughtered by the 'Circle Park Ten.' Perhaps you'd like to say to her that you don't believe her. Go on! Say it right here right now that you don't believe that her daughter was killed in the attack."

Oliver stayed quiet. He didn't want to say it, but a few punches to the gut convinced him otherwise.

"I don't believe you," Oliver said softly.

A collective gasp emanated from the crowd followed by a stunned silence.

"I'm sorry you had to hear that Danielle, but these are the people we're fighting. We have to know what they're like and what they think if we want to stand any chance of beating them. Now, I humbly ask that you consider me when you walk into the polling stations next month so we can finally put an end to this war and bring peace!"

Oliver was then led off of the stage in the same direction he was led on. He tripped and clutched the pants of one of the guards to steady himself. He had just enough mental energy to track his movements and remember from which directions he came.

They're leading me back to the prison. It was nothing but a spectacle. A fucking photo-op.

In his mind, Oliver saw Reece's narrow eyes glistening. They wept blood. The Torch of the Insurrection set the jacket resting on his shoulder alight, engulfing the false determined stare, the cans of food began exploding every which way. Reece turned to face him and shanked his pupils straight through the front of Oliver's head as the whimpering corpse of the boy waddled out of the office and into view. The red chaos of the Insurrection Torch and the black sharpness of the Vigil's ominous *V* danced and swirled together on all of their hands, and led each other in a sinister waltz. Reece's face distorted into a twisted perverted smile and spoke. The camera shutter sounded like a gunshot.

It levels the playing field, friend.

CHAPTER NINE

It hurt to exist when Oliver woke up the next day. Bruises dotted his abdomen and face and he was swelled in areas that he didn't know could swell. He would prefer getting beaten a second time if it meant he could cure himself of the post-beating maladies. Every joint rung out in pain and an unrelenting headache pounded against all sides of his skull. He remained in his cot and stared blankly at the ceiling.

"You awake yet?" Thomas asked.

"Yeah," Oliver replied.

"When they brought you in here you were in a hell of a state. You looked so defeated and empty. Did the sleep help at all?"

"I executed an innocent child and they didn't kill me."

"What?"

"During the raid. I was ordered to execute an innocent child. I listened, and they *didn't* kill me."

"I read that a child was killed in the pamphlet they

brought down that Sunday. I was hoping it wasn't you that did it, but I had my suspicions."

"...they didn't kill me." Oliver repeated softly, not averting his eyes from the partially lit nothing that covered his cell ceiling, "used me as an opportunity..."

Thomas said nothing.

"I would've killed me," Oliver said while rolling over onto his side, "You know I wanted to be just like my father when I was a child. Everything about his life and work seemed admirable and the peak of what it means to be a man. The uniform, the responsibility, the medals for outstanding achievement, the ranks, the respect, the purpose, the simplicity, all of it. It seemed so manageable. The people above you in rank know better than you, and so you listen to them and follow the instructions and you'll succeed. The people below you in rank know worse, and so they need to follow your instructions. Everything and everyone in their places, and you knew your place in it, and were happy with it. There's that structure and the manuals that have every piece of information you'll need in specific and exact detail. You just trained hard and became so competent in your work that you wouldn't have to give any of it a second thought. There was a job well done and a job poorly done. There was no such thing as a job done well for the wrong reasons, or done poorly for the right ones. Nothing to justify or feel sorry for. I haven't spoken to him in over two decades and yet, still, he creeps into my mind when it's quiet. His judgmental face subtly leering at me. Both he and my mother would hate the man I am, and I'd deserve every bit of their ire. Unless they too have been transformed by this war into someone like me. I thought I was doing it *for* something.

For the *good* of some ethereal something. I think that's the worst part of it."

"I think you're one of the better people in the world, Oliver."

"Thomas, I murdered a child. There is no redemption out there for me."

"Trying to craft intelligent sounding excuses used to be your first instinct. It's not anymore. Now you're feeling guiltier, as you should. It's a step. How many people out there even know what the word 'remorse' means nowadays?"

"Remorse isn't good enough," Oliver replied.

"Thinking that is precisely what makes you good enough, not good, but good enough. Better than most others at least."

Oliver remained silent.

"What did they do to you out there?"

"They dragged me to a stage after kicking the shit out of me. Forced me to repeat Insurrection propaganda so they could publicly show they could rebut it pre-election."

"Bastards," Thomas said with a tone of astonishment.

"You said it. The kid's name was Alex and there was no mention of him. They didn't want to blame me for what I did. They wanted a placeholder for the entirety of the Insurrection to beat and berate. Thinking the wrong thing is more of a crime to them than murder."

"You sound different."

"Do I?"

"You're not speaking as technically anymore. Not obsessed with some abstract argument. You talk the way people used to."

"Not sure if that's good or bad. I'm not sure I can go back out there and live. I can see the appeal of being hidden away."

"Do you feel any different?"

"I don't know. I feel..." Oliver paused for a moment. He felt formless. Like a liquid without a container to hold it and so it leaked into whatever crevice ended up coming along.

"...cheated," Oliver finally came out with. He felt the tingling sensation under his eyes and in his cheeks that normally pre-empts tears, but none dripped out.

"I'm tired," Oliver said as he struggled to sit up. He groaned in agony as he lifted himself from his back. He took a few heavy breaths after he forced himself upright. Pain surged through his chest at the peak of each inhalation.

Okay, shallow breathing from here on out.

He lifted up his shirt and started slowly pressing his thumb into the bruises. The intense pain of a pressed bruise would make the constant ache more relative and bearable. He stretched his neck and back despite the ache. He threw his scrawny legs over the side of the cot and stood up on his toes to stretch his legs and crack his ankles.

"Why aren't you more upset with me?" Oliver asked.

"What do you mean?" Thomas replied.

"I'm a murderer."

"No you're not. I don't believe that."

"Yes, I am. I committed murder. It's very simple."

"Did you do it because you wanted to do it?"

"No."

"Okay, well then why did you do it?"

Oliver sighed, "Because I was frightened of what

my commander would do to me if I didn't, and I didn't want to look stupid or wishy-washy in front of him."

"So you're just a coward with an enormous ego. That I *can* forgive."

"Thank you that's enough. But you're not wrong." Oliver said.

One of the fluorescent bulbs outside of the cell went out but not completely. It began flickering and the bright humming white light turned into a soft murmuring purple. There was a momentary vacation from the irritating buzzing and whirring sound, but the subject of annoyance was swiftly replaced by a frustrating clicking and tinging noise. Oliver struggled and limped over to the bars to take a look, and then slowly dragged himself back to the cot. The light was flickering.

"Are they going to fix that?" Oliver asked.

"Probably, they like these bulbs because it disturbs sleep and so leaving them broken for too long might allow their prisoner to comfortably rest."

"Great," Oliver said.

The door swung open upstairs and the guard was bringing down Thomas' daily meal. Only this time he paused for a moment and eyed the broken bulb.

The guard folded his lips inward, "They're not gunna like this." he said in an oddly loud whisper. He must've thought he was saying it under his breath. Thomas got his meal and started to chew.

"Oh, by the way," Thomas started to say with his mouth full, "I saved you some bread from last night because I assumed you'd be pretty hungry and you'll need your strength to recover. So you're getting an extra large portion today."

Thomas threw three generously sized pieces of

bread, five stalks of asparagus, and his freshly cooked baked potato across the tiny hallway and they landed perfectly except for the potato. It rolled a few more inches away from the cell bars.

"Did they make it?" Thomas asked.

"Most of it."

"Most?"

"Yeah, the potato rolled out of my reach," Oliver said in a panicked whisper

"You'd better fucking reach it Oliver."

Oliver stood up and waddled toward the bars. He snatched up the bread and asparagus and laid them down on the cot. He shuffled himself back to the front of the cell and then got on his knees. He squeezed his hand through the cell bars through the intense soreness. He extended his arm as far as it could possibly go and he was still about an entire hand's length away from the morsel.

"I can't get it!" Oliver said in a panic.

"There is no 'can't' here. You have to reach it!" Thomas said with a combination of fear and anger.

Oliver pressed his shoulder and armpit further into the cell bars and screamed as he did so. The pain was excruciating. He was able to get his hand about an inch further out, but still not close enough. He pressed it even further forward and nearly dislocated his shoulder. His body was boiling with pain. What if his arm got stuck? The door upstairs swung open and Oliver quickly retracted his arm and moved over towards the cot. Thomas was absolutely silent.

Maybe they won't see it? It's in the shadow of a busted bulb after all.

A man wearing no helmet came down the stairs. A tool belt at his waist and a replacement bulb was being held like a ceremonial rifle in his left arm. His other arm was carrying a small ladder. A *V* pulsated out of the back of his hand. Initially he didn't see the potato, but when he opened the ladder one of the legs mushed it into the floor. He looked at Thomas' cell, then directly into Oliver's eyes, and then ran back up the stairs, leaving the ladder behind.

"Don't!" Oliver shouted as the man made it halfway up the stairs but there was nothing stopping him. They knew now.

"Thomas I'm so sorry," Oliver said.

"It's alright. Not your fault," Thomas said solemnly. He knew what was coming.

A few minutes later three guards stormed down the stairs. Two were holding cudgels and one was holding a large pocket knife. Over the next twenty minutes Thomas received an even more savage beating than Oliver had the day before. They knocked the wind out of him and so Thomas couldn't even muster a painful wail. He gasped for breath as they smacked him in the face and stomach. Sometimes the gasps would be interrupted by a kick to the ribs. Oliver screamed at the guards even though he knew they couldn't hear him. Thomas stopped making noise but the subtle sound of bones being struck by hard thick plastic still rung out.

The sound of a beating never quite makes clear the true horror of being kicked to shreds by three people who don't really care whether you make it out alive, let alone retain all of your teeth. The guards stopped for about fifteen seconds, and then Thomas let out a scream. The scream was the culmination of every squeal of misery that Thomas never got to express. The pain, loss, and failure of several civilizations were packed into that scream and Oliver could've sworn that the entire building shook as a result. The three men slammed the cell door shut, walked back up the stairs, left bloody partial footprints in the floor, and then slammed that door shut too.

"You okay?" Oliver asked after a bit of time went by.

Thomas didn't respond. All he could do was take deep desperate wheezing breaths. An hour passed without a word. Then another hour. Oliver started pacing around the cell and occasionally struggled to kneel and take a drink of water out of the toilet. After a total of five hours Thomas finally spoke up through coughs, "They did it to me."

"Did what?" Oliver asked.

"They carved a patch off of my right hand. They carved *nothing* out of my skin because I helped you. Took it as a sign of allegiance with the Insurrection."

"Thomas I'm so sorry. This is my fault," Oliver responded.

"No it isn't. I offered the deal up to you in the first place."

"I suppose."

"I wish I could hold someone's hand right about now. They're not going to feed me anymore I know it."

Oliver stopped talking so Thomas could get a few deep gulps of air into his lungs.

Thomas sighed and said, "You know, I thought I would be more upset about having my hand either tattooed or scarred up. But oddly enough I'm not."

"Why?"

"I fell for the same trap that the rest of you fell into, just in a different way. Vigil people get tattooed because they want to permanently display a symbol of their loyalty. You Insurrection guys carve that off and proudly wave your scars around as a symbol of your disloyalty. I wanted to defy all of that. I wanted to be something outside of it all. Something that couldn't be made to take blame for what's happening, and so I was determined to keep my hand the way it was until I died. But therein lies the problem. That's where it is. That's the solution to all of it."

"What's the solution?" Oliver asked with concern.

"It's just a symbol. It's only your hand. It only alters what people perceive us to be, not what we actually are. That's why they jailed me, but still continued to feed me wonderful food. They didn't know what to do with me. They didn't know what the correct moral course of action was because someone like me existing throws off their all-encompassing moralities and doctrines. That's the truth of it. They think they're in my head and in my heart but they aren't. They think they've deciphered my secret loyalty to the Insurrection but they haven't. They genuinely think they are in my head but they're all just lost in their own. Every single person drenched in the war right now says that they want it to end, but there's no way that they actually do. On some level we wanted this to happen because it did, and we want this to keep going because it does. You have no idea the relief I feel at this moment. I no longer have to hold the line for anything. I can rest. I lost."

Oliver got into his cot after eating the food Thomas gave him and tried to sleep, but the aches were making it difficult. Every time he would doze off some god awful sting jolted him back into consciousness. There was no comfortable position anywhere. He tried shriveling up into a ball on his side, lying on his stomach and back, stretching out, and none of it worked.

He wished he still had his journal with him so he

could document everything that was happening to him. The pummeling, constant hunger and worry prevented his mind from retaining most of what went on. He could recall Thomas' stories and his appearance on stage, but the endless boredom and drudgery of prison life was lost from his mind. It wasn't important enough to remember but he wanted to remember it. He wanted to remember everything. He still couldn't recall what his parents voices sounded like. He was already starting to forget the sound of Edward's voice.

It seemed that still no one could remember and adequately back up precisely what happened to the Circle Park Ten. With everything Oliver had seen of the Vigil, he wouldn't be surprised that they shot a whole bunch of peaceful demonstrators for wanting their publication back. He also didn't know whether Insurrection propaganda justified an unprovoked violent act on the part of his side of the war, especially if they were fully stuck in the mindset that he was as he stared Alex in the face. He realized in that moment that he truly had no idea why he thought the Insurrection was a completely innocent party in that conflict for so long, or exactly why he thought anything he had thought for over twenty years.

Exactly how long have I been in here?

"Thomas," Oliver said with a whisper, "Thomas. Thomas, you awake?"

He did not receive a reply. Two hours later a couple of guards came downstairs to check on the poor elderly soul. Oliver heard the cell door squeak open.

"Hey," One of the guards shouted, "Hey!"

There was no response. A couple of soft taps were heard. The sound of an open palm colliding with skin. Then a pause.

"Nope," the other said.

The guards grabbed Thomas by the ankles and dragged him out of his cot. They treated his body like a piece of broken furniture. His back was being scraped across the floor as they moved him into the hallway. The cell door was shut. Thomas' body was then hauled up the stairs by two men who thought they'd merely killed another enemy combatant. Oliver was able to see him for the first time. His nose was oddly small for an older man. He had short stringy dark grey hair that bundled toward the sides and back of his head leaving only a few long wisps on top. Very pronounced laugh lines were carved into his face and he was still quite full and healthy looking despite his imprisonment. He was yanked up the stairs by his feet as the back of his head smacked each stair as the guards ascended, and the thick metal door was closed gently behind them. The flickering light in the hallway went out completely, and the last existing piece of impartial sentience eventually found its corpse buried beneath the Earth.

CHAPTER TEN

Oliver had been alone for four days when the rumbling began. He dropped to the floor and placed his ear against it as his eyes darted about the cell. The first subtle vibrations weren't much of anything and he thought it was just the subway speeding underneath him, but this was the first time he felt these miniature tremors and thought that perhaps their origin was a bit less conventional and routine.

It was a welcome problem. His mind craved work. It craved some sort of preoccupation that wasn't to do with his shouting stomach and crippling boredom. Anything to avoid the desperate need for the body to vomit while empty. The shakes and low hums started small and were only noticeable if Oliver stood still, shut his eyes, focused his ears, and quieted his thoughts. Over time they grew in frequency and intensity. It began to sound like a thunderstorm outside, but the noises were too short and snappy to conclude as such. Thunder roars slowly, but these sounds were more instant and defined. They began to get louder and the room shook even more.

An enormous force slammed in close proximity to Oliver's cell. The whole room shook as if it was at the center of an earthquake and he was knocked to the floor. His ears were ringing due to the booming snap and subsequent loud low bellow that gently faded over time. This was a familiar experience. He felt this way a long time ago, and Oliver's subconscious poked him with the answer to the searing question.

Bombs. Artillery? Have they truly made it this far inward?

The explosions kept raining down and all Oliver could do was sit in the corner and hope the roof didn't give way and crush him to death. After a few minutes he dove under his cot. It wasn't much protection, but it was better than nothing.

I just want to be away from this. Anything but this.

He closed his eyes. He imagined himself on a steep hill overlooking the entirety of Insurrection and Vigil territory with a clear sky during sunrise. The bustle of war reduced to inconsequential blips on a planetary scale. He could judge it all and play chess master. Each drop in the ocean being thousands of deaths and feeling nothing. Treat it as a minor setback that had to be dealt with by the replacement of expendable flesh. It would be better than this hounding remorse, this bloodthirsty wolf chasing him through the chasms of his head that could only be heeled and caged through daily drudgery or bone-snapping stress. He wanted a normal day.

The door at the top of the stairs began clanking and smacking as two men wearing Insurrection jackets forced it open and descended into the prison hallway.

They were checking all of the cells and Oliver kept quiet. There was no feeling of comradery left within him for he had never met those two men. He knew nothing of what they were like and what sinister potential they had stored away for situations like this, plus this structure had been pretty sturdy during the attack and being out there would only open him up to more peril. The two revolutionaries finally reached his cell. One of the men pointed his rifle at him through the bars.

"Hand!" The other man ordered.

Oliver stuck his hand out from underneath the cot and presented his scar.

"Alright, let's get him outta here."

The two men then took out a set of keys and tried a few of them before they'd found the correct one. They assisted Oliver upright and held his arms as they walked him up the stairs.

"You okay?" one of the men asked.

"Yes," Oliver said, "Just hungry, and want to be away from all this."

They shut the door behind them. There were holes blasted in the building. Remnants of office appliances, broken glass, and pieces of scorched paper peppered the floor. Dead guards littered the area. The short vindictive guard that ordered his beating was slouched against a wall with his eyes half open with blood dripping from his mouth and neck. He felt no satisfaction upon being greeted with the demise of his former tormentor. As they walked his bare foot scraped across a small piece of glass, but he was too tired and deadened to worry about it. Flames spurted from the holes in the walls, and the sound of bursting bombs was accompanied by the cracking of burning wood which sent flurries of sparks twisting in the cold night sky. It was a harrowing monument to the mating of fire and flesh.

The heat hurt his eyes and he was forced to shut them as they crossed through the searing doorways. They reached the front door of the building and a gust of freezing wind brushed against his face. For a split second he saw every horror that lies within the human spirit laid out before him on the ground beneath his prison's front steps.

The nearly dead screeched for a few more moments of life. Their faces melted off, men with huge smiles on their faces executed frail and frightful women and children, bullets were rammed through the guts of innocent men, other men laughed and set buildings alight with flamethrowers and gasoline, the stench of carcasses permeated the air and a chorus of tearful bloody sputtering assaulted the ears.

Oliver felt nothing about this. Everything inside of him had collapsed. He chose to look up and admire the unpredictable beauty of the fire whipping out from the tops of buildings in front of a starry black sky. It was as if a dragon had finally been awakened from its ancient slumber and was sent to purify the entire world of its innocence. It was all real. It was all happening right in front of him. None of the pamphlets or speeches could capture the utter depravity of this scene.

One of the men pulled out a radio, "Bring it around," he said into it.

"What's it?" Oliver asked.

"Evacuation. We're getting you home, friend."

"How many like me have you found so far?"

"None, just you. All the others were gone or dead."

A truck that looked similar to the one he drove out

to the Divide in pulled up, but this time it had a proper cover for the seating area in the back. They loaded Oliver in and then he was driven off. Two trained medical personnel began running diagnostics on him.

"Foot and food," Oliver said.

They began wrapping up the laceration on the bottom of his foot. One of the medics pulled a small packet of crackers out of his pocket and gave them to him. Oliver scarfed these down quickly, shuffled himself toward the front of the vehicle, slid onto the floor, and rested his head up against the wall that divided the back from the driver. He let out an enormous sigh.

"Liquor?" Oliver asked.

"Why would we have that?" The medic responded

"Do you have anything to kill this pain?" Oliver pointed to his foot.

"No, sorry. Used all our morphine in the attack."

"Alright."

Through the rectangular open hole Oliver could see the terrible slideshow of death getting smaller and smaller as the truck sped away. The only thing that he could feel was the intense bumping of the truck that made it difficult for him to rest his muscles anywhere. His eyes drooped and he started studying his body. He was covered with splats of grey grime. He stank for numerous awful reasons. He lost a lot of weight. One of the medics took his Insurrection jacket off and draped it over Oliver. It felt much heavier than usual, and he felt even dirtier with it on, but he accepted the offer.

Edward

A tiny warm feeling radiated through his chest and his head began to feel a lot lighter. He'd be able to see Edward's reaction when he walked into the apartment building. He imagined Edward's broken smile and tears of joy in knowing that he was still alive. How worried must he have been? Relief rushed through his body as the torturous scene dwindled over the horizon as they exited the city. The soft orange glow of the fire resembled the last few moments of a sunset, and Oliver stared at it, admired it, and ignored the gross reality lurking beneath it.

"What did they do to you in there?" One medic asked with child-like curiousness.

"Enough. They did enough." Oliver said.

"Oh come on! Indulge me," the medic said.

"They killed my friend."

"My word, bet you're glad we showed up huh?"

"Yeah"

"Good thing we're finally beating those bastards back and gaining some ground. When's the last time Nicholas got something like this done? Years?"

"Good thing," Oliver repeated.

"You okay?"

"Yeah"

"Doesn't sound like it. Anyhow, just know that we're winning now."

"Yeah, I saw out there what victory looks like."

"Buck up, this is what all of us have been dreaming of for decades."

Oliver hung his head, "I suppose it is. A little warmer than I imagined it. Not as green."

"Why don't you get some rest?" the medic said, brushing his statement off as delusion due to hunger and fatigue.

"Good idea," Oliver said and closed his eyes. The ragged and cratered ground prevented him from sleeping. On a few occasions he even had his head slammed against the wall of the truck.

After around four hours of driving they reached the Divide again. This time there were Insurrection soldiers stationed in the watchtowers. The two medics leaned a ladder up against the wall and Oliver struggled over it. Another vehicle was waiting on the other side.

Oliver was packed into the back, mushing himself up against the shoulder of a man who had his foot torn apart by a fragmentation grenade. The white ball of gauze covering where his foot should've been was bloody near to the point of leaking. It looked like someone just balled up all of his foot's innards and wrapped them like a misshapen birthday present.

The first signs of civilization started to appear as they approached a city. They were finally able to use a smooth functioning street. A couple of abandoned gas stations and outdated toll booths flew by. The painkillers had begun to wear off the other men as Oliver was dropped off at a civilian bus station in the middle of an empty highway parking lot.

The men shifted from joyous sighing to groaning in agony as the truck sped away, presumably to a hospital. Eight other people were waiting for the bus to arrive and would stare at Oliver's tattered body and clothes when he wasn't looking. He knew they were looking at him. He could feel the hot beam of their eyes on the back of his head. He didn't have the energy to care, all petty social anxieties fade away when one is exhausted, starving, and in pain. The red and brown bus turned into the parking lot. A red torch had been spray painted on the sides, but one could see tiny remnants of the old blue-grey paint where the job was botched. In yellow-orange lights on a small screen read: "oo: Circle Park"

Oliver tried to shuffle his way to the front, but the others were already standing in front of the small doorway. The driver was checking everyone's ticket. He was a very bottom-heavy man wearing an Insurrection jacket. He had a body that fit a profession which required him to be on his ass all day.

I wonder if the job makes them fat or if they screen for fatness during the interview.

Oliver didn't have a ticket and it was his turn at the front.

"Ticket?" the man asked with a gruff voice.

"I don't have one I just came from…"

"No ticket can't let you on the bus."

"You didn't let me finish I…"

"And you didn't hear me the first time. No ticket can't let you on."

The driver turned around and walked back to his seat.

Oliver started yelling, "I got back from the war! Nobody told you I'd be here? I was called for service through the Emergency Protocol! The Vigil locked me in a cell for months and I'm trying to get home!"

"Someone *is* supposed to tell me that. I thought you were homeless, my mistake. Get on board."

Oliver stepped onto the bus. The driver turned around and said, "Ladies and gentlemen, we have a veteran from the war here. Show him some respect and let him sit where he wants. You've done us a great service!"

No, please don't.

The crowd applauded as Oliver walked to the back of the bus and sat down in a row with two empty seats. They don't know of anything he did and yet they're clapping. Would they debase themselves like that if they knew precisely what he had done and went through in all of its detail, all the way down to the last stray spark and spittle of blood? They were a bunch of cashiers, middle managers, stockroom workers, and truck drivers casually wishing destruction on half of the world over dinner. Nothing crossed their minds aside from boiling hatred for the Vigil, the mental deadening that came with the drudgery of work, and short blips of true joy during the big moments in the lives of their children and when good news came down about the status of the revolution.

The bus turned in a loop along an elevated highway and entered the bus station near Circle Park. It pulled up inside of a cylindrical parking garage and the entrance to the station was all glass, to include the doors. A small circular sign stood at the end of the parking spot with the number 14 printed in black letters. Two men inside of a glass security office were arguing with one another about something. They were swinging their hands around and yelling, but Oliver couldn't hear any of it. Everyone exited the bus in a cordial fashion, but two bulky Insurrection soldiers stopped him before he could get into the station, "If you'll please follow us we have some things to take care of before we let you back in."

The two men led Oliver into a very standard looking office behind a pair of locked double doors on the station's lower level. It looked like Oliver was getting a loan. Clean white walls with bland artwork on them, a soft carpet on the ground, metal and plastic chairs, a desk piled up with paperwork, a few stamps, and a small cup for pens. The two guards left the office and Oliver was sitting there with the office worker alone. He was a tinier man, but had very stern eyes and a deep voice. The man coughed.

"If you'll answer my questions quickly and honestly we can be done with this. Reece has instituted a new questionnaire that we are required to ask returning prisoners of war before they can be readmitted into the Insurrection."

"Reece? What did Nicholas have to say about this?"

"Are you a loyalist?" The man asked with suspicion. Now was not the time for questions.

"No, I've just been gone for a while and I was a bit confused. Nicholas was running things when I was sent out."

"Nicholas has been banished from Insurrection territory for being a useful idiot for the Vigil. Reece has taken over and has led us to more victories in a few months than Nicholas had in a few years. Only the diehard loyalists joined him in his banishment, but most likely they're all already dead from the cold and hunger."

Oliver sunk in his chair, "I had no idea."

"Onto the questions, were you exposed to Vigil propaganda during your time as a prisoner?"

"Yes,"

"Did you find any of it interesting?"

Oliver lied, "No, just a bunch of lies."

"Where was the prison located?"

"I...I honestly don't know. It was a few hours away from the Divide based on the return trip, and I got rescued during an attack on the city."

"Okay, that could be a few places but it narrows it down. What is your feeling regarding the mission of the Insurrection?"

Oliver lied, "I fully support a complete military and ideological victory over The Vigil."

"Okay excellent," the office worker scribbled some things.

"Did you ever pretend to be sympathetic to the Vigil's cause to avoid physical or mental torture?"

"No"

"How did you survive then?"

"Someone helped me."

"Was this person Insurrection or Vigil?"

"An Insurrection spy was able to provide me with extra food and delay my execution," Oliver lied.

"Well, good on him. What was his name?"

"Thomas."

"Thomas what?"

"I don't know."

"Smart of him. Not giving you his full name. Well alright. Thank you for your time. We're done here. Please report to your former position of work at the beginning of next month at 0700. Use your free time to rest."

The man stamped the word *Approve* in red on a *Request for Readmission* form, copied it, and then handed the copy to Oliver.

"Thank you," Oliver said as he exited the office. He walked across the bleached clean hallway floor to get to the subway section of the station. There were remains of Nicholas posters that were torn down where the paper was weaker than the adhesive, and the shards that were left looked like bright white claws. Next to them were plastered propaganda posters for the Insurrection featuring the photo Oliver took for Reece. A red frame with a light brown trim surrounded the cropped photo and the words, "Forward to a Brighter Future" were written at the bottom in sharp black lettering. No mention of the dead bodies. No mention of Alex.

Oliver looked around to make sure it was safe because he desperately wanted to tear the poster off of the wall, but there were too many witnesses. He left the photo hanging there wishing he could turn it into ash with his eyes.

PART 3

CHAPTER ELEVEN

THE SOUNDS OF RUSTED METAL RUBBING AGAINST more rusted metal pierced Oliver's ears as he exited the tunnel through a staircase to the street. It was that horrific bat-like high pitched squeal that made the ears tingle and the neck tense up. He walked slowly over to his apartment building, passing by previously worn out buildings that had since been renovated. The enormous hole in his wall appeared to have been patched up as well. It finally looked like a home should look. A shrine dedicated to comfort and safety. A place where humans live.

He strode through the front door and into the hallway. Desperately, he wanted to sit in his apartment and sink into his chair, dissolve into it and become part of the scenery, but Edward needed him, and he needed Edward. Oliver shuffled over to Edward's door and knocked on it.

"Sorry, I'm not taking appointments right now. Try again in a few weeks." Edward said.

"Okay, Edward, I'll just go upstairs then." Oliver replied and laughed.

Sounds of papers thrashing and knick-knacks clanging to the floor rung out.

Edward opened his front door and hugged his friend. He wept and covered Oliver's ripped shirt with mucus, tears, and dribble. It was the first display of true human tenderness he'd received in what felt like years.

"I knew it. There was no way," Edward struggled to say through his tears.

Oliver returned his embrace and did his best not to cry. Edward wasn't like everyone else here. Sure, he believed in everything they believed and said the very same things that they said. His mind had been molded into a monstrosity by the war, but his heart was too strong to be moved to true hatred. Oliver's heart had been moved, so in essence, he was the weaker man. The smarter man, but the weaker man.

"It's so good to see you again," Oliver said, taking in Edward's new look. He'd grown patchy facial hair and hadn't cut his hair in months.

"What happened to you? Where were you?"

"Later," Oliver said. "We can talk later about that."

"Okay...so much has happened since you left," Edward said and ushered Oliver into his apartment, "Nicholas was banished and his op-ed writer Reece took over. He's renovating all of the buildings out here. He's given a whole bunch of great speeches. People have more money to spend now on frivolous things like pictures of their families so my business has been soaring. I always knew you'd make it back. I never lost hope. Not even for a minute. I've been making a bit of extra money so I bought you a couch upstairs. I still don't have enough for a bed, but the couch should be more comfortable than that that dreadful chair. Do you..."

Edward wiped his nose, "Do you remember when you said you wanted to start your own pamphlet? Well take a look at this!"

Edward handed him a piece of paper. It was a pamphlet cover page with a black and white photo of Oliver sitting at his desk in the library looking up at the television in the corner. In red letters above the picture was printed, "The Oliver Column."

"I wasn't sure what you'd want to call it. You don't have to use that title if you don't want to. I couldn't come up with anything cool or catchy or anything like that. It's not a huge deal if you think the name for it isn't great. I can even change the picture if it's not to your tastes. In fact, tomorrow we can..."

"Edward," Oliver said, "Thank you."

"You're welcome," Edward replied, "Also I was saving this for when you got back!"

Edward jogged over to his fridge and took out a bottle of bourbon, "I was able to afford this with my earnings from the week after you left. It's not the greatest quality in the world, but it's not the worst either. What do you say?"

"I need to change first. Pour me a glass. I'd love some," Oliver said.

"Sure! Go ahead. I hope you don't mind I got you new clothes upstairs."

I need to pretend the world is just us for a bit. Sleep. Won't be able to sleep. The bourbon will help. It better help.

Oliver entered his apartment and everything was cleaned and renovated aside from his chair and the stack of Weekly Reports in the corner. On his new off-white couch was a pair of thick checkered flannel pajama pants with the string belt missing. Edward must have picked these up from a thrift shop somewhere.

How long have these been sitting here?

Oliver changed into them and headed back to Edward's apartment.

"Here, take this," Edward said as he handed his uniform jacket to Oliver.

Oliver threw the jacket over himself and sat on Edward's raggedy loveseat.

"Why didn't you replace this awful thing?" Oliver asked.

"Only had enough in the budget for one new couch I'm afraid," Edward said as he brought over two very full glasses. Edward spun a spindly wooden chair around and sat across from Oliver. They both proceeded to take large gulps from their glasses.

"How was it?" Edward said.

"Oh it was fine. A little too much kick on the finish, but I'll get used to it."

"No, the war! The mission. How are we doing?"

Oliver slumped in his chair a bit, "We're doing fine." He looked down at the amber liquid and sloshed it around in the glass.

"You don't seem very enthusiastic," Edward said.

"If I don't seem that way it's because I'm not."

"What happened to you?"

"Can't we do this later? Can't I just sit here with you and enjoy the drink you got me?"

Edward stood up, his eyes filled with fear and his hands shaking slightly, "You know what? No. We can't do this later. You were gone for months! I'm your friend and I've been your friend since we both joined the Insurrection. I'm not your baby brother alright? I am entitled to some answers from you. Do you have any idea what it was like not having anyone here, ever? Not knowing whether your only friend has been blown to bits, tortured, or lost in the cold?"

I guarantee I suffered way more than you did.

Oliver sighed, "You're right. I'm sorry. I'll tell you everything. You don't have to be scared of me Edward. You're my only living friend too."

Edward sat down, embarrassed with himself, "Okay. Thank you."

After briefing Edward on everything that happened, the two of them finished their third glass of bourbon. Oliver was happy to be in the present moment, but couldn't fully pull himself away from everything that had happened and the new questions that had been branded on his mind.

"Do you remember anything from Circle Park?" Oliver asked.

"No, I didn't live near the area. Didn't have my camera then either. I was too young. I knew what the papers and TV news were saying about it, but I wasn't there."

"All I remember is gunshots. I don't know where they came from, who shot the weapons, or anything. But for some reason that sound rings out in my head whenever I think about it. I'm sitting at my desk as a child, and loud 'bangs' drew my attention to the window. But I must not have had a decent view of the incident because nothing else comes up."

"Could it have been anything else? Like, not gunfire?"

"Perhaps, do you think proving what actually happened could end the war?"

"I have no idea. This war is everything now. This

war *is* the world that everyone lives in. To end the war now would be to, in essence, end the world."

"What if the world could *truly* be different though? If I can figure out what genuinely happened in Circle Park we would know who to blame."

"Where did you get all of this stuff? Why are you speaking so oddly?"

Oliver's eyes began to widen, "Something happened, and they both believe the opposite occurred with the exact same data, but we no longer have the data. We need it. We need something proving one side in this war wrong once and for all or else the death will continue."

"You've lost me," Edward said.

"All this time it's been eluding me, but I think I've figured it out. The whole goddamned thing."

"I hope you're right."

"Me too."

Two more drinks. Oliver coughed from the electric sting that erupted from his throat into his nose.

"What have you been doing since I was gone?" Oliver asked.

"Well, you know mostly this," Edward pointed to the camera sitting on his desk.

"I don't think I've ever asked you what made you pick up photography," Oliver said.

"You haven't. You've always been too wrapped up in these grand schemes of yours."

Oliver laughed and lurched forward in his chair, wobbling as he did so, "What got you so interested in photography?"

"I was always so confused about things," Edward started looking very somber and Oliver's smile subsided, "Everybody was always screaming and yelling and telling me different things. I'm not stupid. I'm just... confused. The camera is never confused though. It always captures exactly what you see at the time you take it. You can look at a photo that you took and say 'that happened' and know it for sure."

"I see your point, Oliver said. "I don't see how anyone forced into these circumstances can trust anyone."

"You weren't forced. You joined."

Oliver put his glass on the floor, closed his eyes, and rubbed the space between his eyebrows, "I know that."

"I'm sorry if I've upset you. I'm not trying to argue with you."

"I know."

"Please don't be upset."

"I'm not. I'm frustrated. I just need to prove what happened in Circle Park."

"We're doing fine as it is. We're winning the war. What Advantage does discovering the 'truth' about Circle Park really give us?"

"Edward, we'll know it! It doesn't matter if not a single person on Earth believes us. We will know. Even if it's impossible to express the truth in words we'll know deep in our heads what is real and what isn't. Does that not tempt you a little bit?"

"Where is all of this coming from? This type of stuff never convinced anyone before the war and it won't convince anyone now."

"The man I met in prison knew nothing of the war and was only allowed Vigil propaganda. He believed nothing about the incident and was satisfied with that. He never had the opportunity to figure it out and didn't even want one. But I've been given that opportunity now and I can't let it waste away."

Edward leaned back in his chair and hunched his back. He looked at the floor. Edward doubted his friend for the first time. The transformation Oliver underwent in prison was deep and cataclysmic.

"You've gone mad," Edward said.

"No, I *was* mad."

"Alright, what do you want me to do?" Edward said with timidity.

"Nothing, I just needed to tell someone and you're all I have."

The two men talked gleefully into the early morning as if nothing of note had happened, laughed at jokes that weren't very funny, made fun of each other's faces, and marveled at how half a year seemed like a grand stretch of time. They finished their glasses and embraced again. Oliver went upstairs and did not sleep, captivated by the possibility that everything he thought he knew was a lie.

CHAPTER TWELVE

Oliver pushed through the growing throng of people who gathered there each morning and used his key to get in. It was the familiar smell as he entered the library that most depressed him. The sinister stench of mildew being a telltale sign of the rotting corpses of books. Crumpled pamphlets were strewn around at the base of the bookshelves, under the desks, and the few trashcans in the room were overflowing with dead paper stained by finger-oils.

He spent around an hour cleaning the hardwood floors. He emptied the trashcans into a dumpster around the side of the building. There were so many things that needed to be done here that his replacement had ignored. The person taking his job while he was away should've been there by now. Someone had left a large half-empty paper cup filled with what Oliver could only presume was at one point something drinkable. But now it had grown its own ecosystem and it reeked of stale vinegar and illness. The bottom of the cup had grown soft and malleable as if eaten through by the pure toxicity of the contents.

He disposed of it in the bathroom, dumping the thick diseased liquid down the drain and running hot water through the pipes, hoping to scald all of those pestilent fungi to death. He then ripped up the paper cup using toilet paper as gloves and, one by one, flushed the pieces down the toilet.

Excitement boiled in his arteries. Today was the day he was going to find the answer everyone desperately needed, but never bothered to search for.

All of the people clamoring for a sparse update on the war have no clue about the intellectual roots of this conflict because they're fully involved. They have a stake in the answer, and as such, fear its discovery. But why fear the discovery of the answer to a question that you believe to already be answered?

If one believes that Insurrection bodies are the only corpses in those graves, then what's the harm in confirming it? Ah, there's the issue sprawled out naked for each side of this war to witness. They fear it because while they profess to be convinced of something, they are not. They either lie to convince others of lies, or are trying to convince themselves to believe something they know they have no reason to believe.

With this revelation Oliver uncovered his own faults. For decades he felt strongly about things he was completely ignorant of. Only an outside voice could rule on this matter, but there were none. Not a single human being in the country lacked a preference in regard to the answer. Even Oliver preferred there to be only Insurrection bodies buried in Circle Park because it would confirm his former beliefs about the event, and that's what everyone wanted at the time. They wanted their own beliefs confirmed, and yet two mutually exclusive beliefs could not truly be confirmed simultaneously. But it was made so.

One half of the country believes the total contradiction of the other half. It's not the facts that mattered so much, but the contradiction itself. Being incorrect was a much more forgivable offense than being perceived a traitor in the growing conflict. It was all rhetoric passionately making cases for things, but based on what?

The truth is so weak, but so precious. It has such thin armor. A stray book translator caught up in a political treatise they'd recently read tweaking a few troublesome paragraphs, a non-fiction writer looking for a way to spice up the story to keep his audience interested, an avoidable misinterpretation making it into an official textbook, an awkward paraphrasing, a politically convenient stripping of context. All of these things might kill the truth forever. One careless flick of the pen mixed with disinterest and it's all over.

Alter the course of an airplane by a mere one or two degrees and one will end up miles away from their original destination and the distance only increases with the amount of time travelled. Turn one or two degrees in the other direction and the two vessels will be even further away from one another, yet both believe they've arrived at the same place. What happened happened, what is happening is happening, and no amount of disbelief piled onto it by the human species will render those truths lifeless. Weak, yes. Frail, obviously. Useless, perhaps in a grim way. But never dead. There's always a chance to revive it. A slim chance, but a chance nonetheless. Sure, alter the course of the plane and arrive at a lie. It doesn't mean the expected destination has vanished into non-existence, it just means that no human will ever believe it exists for the rest of time eternal.

The routine was done. Walk outside, grab heavy paper, close heavy door, unwrap and stack pamphlets, open the doors, endure complaints, clean up after everyone leaves after twenty minutes. Not a single person had noticed he returned. There was no, "Oh hey, you're back" or any of that. He wondered whether his replacement had to stomach the pomposity of library goers just as much. The state he found the library in convinced him that whoever was working here was too uncaring to worry about complaints.

Oliver rose from his desk and cautiously made his way toward the "History" section of the library. He didn't bother with the television. One bottom shelf all the way to the left had multiple volumes of a series called, "History in Decades." Oliver squatted down to read the spines. They had books that covered the 1930s all the way through to the 2020s. There existed no history on the 2030s, 2040s, or 2050s. The writing down of history became a useless exercise when the war began. Oliver grabbed the "2020s" book and as he walked back to his desk he gently wiped the dust from the front cover. His heart began racing.

He sat down at his desk and started hungrily scanning the pages for anything about Circle Park. He wasn't sure of the exact year that it happened and so he had to look at everything. He passed by the fracturing of the political parties, the proposition to maintain the general party structure but rename them, a few of the larger scale bombing efforts by domestic revolutionary groups, lists of politicians that supported or denounced violence from various factions, all the way through to the eventual tattooing policy and the shutting down of Internet access for civilians.

This was only accomplished through each side of the political divide back then believing that their opponents were being radicalized via the Internet. They were both willing to sacrifice, well, make the civilian population sacrifice, their freedoms so long as it meant that the enemy's ability to disseminate propaganda was hindered. Most of the population got on board and preferred to suppress their own well-being if it meant the suppression of their opponents as well in lieu of defending their own well-being and, in tandem, their opponents. They were perfectly willing to uproot the economy of the country as well, businesses collapsed left and right, the largest companies were exclusively Internet-based and everything tumbled down.

Pet enemies were blamed for everything, what eventually became the Vigil blamed the Insurrection and what eventually became the Insurrection blamed the Vigil. The Insurrection called the Vigil hypocritical for supporting the amendments and motions that caused this while at the same time, the Vigil condemned the Insurrection for supporting the amendments and motions, or at least, providing the circumstances that required the Vigil to support them. There was no discussion of "side-effects" or alternative logical consequences. Everyone was focused on the end goal. Win. Win. Win. Win. Oliver read of a popular political slogan from back then:

'No citizen has the right to be wrong.'

So who was *actually* wrong? There was nothing about Circle Park in the books. Not even in passing was this pivotal moment mentioned. Did it happen in the 2030s? Must have. No, definitely late 2020s because he remembered he was still in elementary school. Did three decades honestly bleed together so smoothly? It's possible that only a sophisticated class of leader knows what happened. People like Nicholas, Reece, and that smooth condescending baritone on stage. The other more frightening possibility was that no one truly knew. Not a single person alive knew what the hell this war was all about, why it began, their motives within it, what was happening, and why they believed anything.

Oliver put the book away and began leafing through other random tomes in the same section hoping to find some answer to the burning question but found nothing. No photographs, no statements, no witnesses, nothing. Oliver then realized the purposelessness and illogical nature of his search. How did he know that the compilers of this history didn't have skin in the game? How did he know they didn't leave the event out on purpose because it portrays them in a bad light? How could he possibly trust anything he hadn't seen and felt with his own senses? If, for the last three decades, one side of this conflict had built itself on a lie, would they not do everything in their power to preserve their narrative? Who in their right mind would write down things they disbelieve in as recorded history? Too many questions and no resolution.

Oliver put his elbows on the desk and pressed his palms against his temples. Hours upon hours of tiresome research and he was no closer to discovering the truth about that day. He realized that he wouldn't have believed what the books said no matter what was written down due to the potential for malicious bias creeping its way in.

Was there no way to find this out? Had this event truly been lost to history, only existing as a fractured memory in the minds of human beings? It happened three decades ago. It's not like he'd be able to find camera footage or any kind of physical evidence as to whether the Insurrection story or the Vigil story was accurate here, and who potentially could receive the blame for plunging the country into war. His brain was not wired for this kind of thought work. He knew the answer existed but he had no way of knowing what was needed to discover it. The books held nothing of significance. As quickly as he'd dreamed up this plan, he discarded it.

The brutal judgment was branded on his heart in that moment. He was a wicked man starved of the opportunity for redemption. This potential discovery was his final distraction, the last chance he would've gotten to describe himself in positive terms. He could've furthered the argument, uttered a definitive sentencing of the state of the world, and be able to maintain his belief that he is contributing to something uplifting and greater than himself. All of this tumbled haphazardly to the library floor as the realization forced its way to the forefront of his mind. He no longer had the capacity to determine fact from fiction unless he experienced an event himself, even then it all depended on his memory holding steady.

He couldn't trust the books, he couldn't trust other people, he couldn't trust the pamphlets, and he couldn't even trust his moderate to long-term memories. As such, the obsession about the war gave way to an obsession over his own sordid nature. How perfectly he fell in line for so long. How powerless he truly was. What a rotten child and man he has been. The lack of redeeming qualities. Slowly and painfully he agonized over his indiscretions, examining himself as if he were judging the character of another man, and found himself wanting. All of his illusions had been broken the moment he accepted that he was incapable of knowing the truth, and in such incapability, could no longer in good conscience side with the Vigil or the Insurrection for fear that he'd choose the wrong one. Yet he realized that without war's tempting justifications and the seductive whistles of false empowerment he was worse than nothing. He was a small evil stain on the Earth's crust.

The answer mattered not any longer, for in his moments of evil, he was not being evil for noble purposes. All of his cruel actions came about through fear and ambition. The truth would not stop anyone from being afraid or craving power, and it's those causes from which moral depravity arises. A combination of fear, power worship, and the forever unmentioned base desire in all human beings to do wicked things to people who they feel deserve it.

The doors to the library creaked open.

"Where the hell have you been?" Oliver asked the portly man shuffling his way to the librarian's desk.

"Who do you think you are?" the man snorted.

"I work here, but I'm on vacation."

"Doesn't look like it."

"Whatever, I don't give a shit." Oliver sighed as he stood up and gave the chair to his replacement.

Oliver heard the man mumble, "That's right, fuck off."

The man yelled at him as he walked out of the library, "Hell of a mess you're leaving, asshole!"

As soon as he got home he started finishing the bottle of bourbon alone in his room, drinking hard and well into the evening, relishing the deadening liquid soaking into the blood brain barrier. He was no longer shackled by Reece's philosophy or by the war, but there was no one to express this to who could understand and no one to tell him where to start. It's like he was holding millions of dollars in the currency of a dead civilization, or had picked open the locked coffin he was buried in.

CHAPTER THIRTEEN

OLIVER OPENED HIS EYES, SLAMMED THEM SHUT again and groaned in pain. His cheek was pressed against the hardwood floor and drool was leaking out of the side of his mouth. There was a stinging tension in his neck and music was playing through the television. His body was facing the television, but his head was resting on the opposite shoulder. As he rose to his feet he started to get lightheaded and trace amounts of tunnel vision, but the arm of the recliner provided a decent grounding point. The thumping in his skull and dried out mouth propelled him towards the faucet. Like a stray cat, he tilted his head sideways and gulped down the water for a few minutes, savoring the tangy metal flavor of it and pausing only to exhale and inhale deeply.

He shut the water off, grabbed the broken porcelain with both hands, and began wretching. He emptied his stomach into the sink and turned the water on to wash the disgusting mixture of liquor and bile down the drain. Every joint ached and his head was still half-swimming in a pool of bourbon, and as if by miracle, it hadn't killed him as he hoped it might've. The thought of going back to work repulsed him, and so he decided that his small act of protest would be to refuse to work at the library when the time came. He just wouldn't show up, and tell no one about it.

Oliver shuffled out of his apartment door and made his way downstairs, gripped the railing with both hands as he did so, and knocked on Edward's door.

"Hey, do you have time to go somewhere?" Oliver shouted through the scratched wood.

"Huh? Where?" Edward responded as he opened the door.

"Where'd you get the bourbon?"

"You ran out already?"

"Yeah"

Edward's shoulders slumped, "I was hoping you'd savor it a bit. That cost me a decent amount of money you know."

"I'm a very quick savorer...sorry."

"No big deal, anyways, I could do with a day off. We'll go to a place I found while you were gone."

Edward organized his desk for a few moments, and then led Oliver out the front door.

It was dusk.

Did I seriously sleep for that long? Or stay up that late?

The overcast was oddly thin this evening and the sleepy colors of the sun could be seen radiating in a soft semi-circle over the horizon. The grainy purples, oranges, and reds filtering through the clouds looked like an old photograph that had been colorized and stained every surface with a comforting warm tint. The dulled hues poked through holes in the fresh scaffolding of new construction projects that were long overdue. At last someone was doing something about the hideous roofs of these tall blown out buildings. They were an absolute eye-sore and did nothing but cast a somber shadow over the city.

Life was bright and out of character in their neighborhood. He wished he could appreciate this new found hope that the folks around him were enjoying, but he couldn't. As they strolled through the area they passed by formerly abandoned shops falling under new management. A few tattered "grand opening" signs were hanging in front of thin but tall buildings offering uniform repair services, cigarettes, coffee, sandwiches, propaganda posters for interior decoration, and furniture. There hadn't been a very stable business in the area for a while, and all of the shop owners were wearing genuine smiles trying to get their stores organized for customers.

"When did all this start?" Oliver asked Edward.

"Honestly, just after Nicholas got ousted. We can actually boast now about making decent progress getting ourselves off of the rationing system. Unfortunately the closest place we can buy food is two train rides away, and even then that's only a produce grocer. But butchers have opened up as well. Even heard there were a few bakeries opening up further down the subway line. With the acquisition of all this new territory we're able to do a lot more than we were previously. Plus, as the pamphlet said a few weeks ago, if we're to continue at this pace the war could be won in about twenty years."

"What is Reece expecting? We'll beat them back enough until there's a surrender."

"Oh no, not that at all. Reece has stated that he

refuses to accept surrender even if it is unconditional. It's his belief that we will need to be on constant alert in case they attempt a resurgence. So after the war is won, much of our forces will spend their time trying to root out the inevitable underground guerillas that will try to take power again."

"Of course…" Oliver said, "What are your thoughts on that?"

"I mean, I'm sure they wouldn't hesitate to do the same to us."

"But you don't know that."

"What?"

"You don't…" Oliver paused because they were passing by a group of people and he didn't want to be overheard, "You don't know that though."

"What? How so?"

"How do you know that the Vigil wouldn't accept an unconditional surrender?" Oliver asked.

"What reason is there to believe that they would?" Edward asked in return.

"Whatever. I guess none. I guess fucking none." Oliver said.

"Why are you so angry about this?"

"Not angry. You're right. No reason to suspect the Vigil wouldn't kill us all." Oliver said in a stern monotone voice.

Edward went quiet and frowned, looked to the pavement, and dropped his shoulders as they continued walking down the sidewalk. There was no way for Oliver to express this urgent aching feeling in his stomach. All the same, Edward was entirely correct when he said that the Vigil would, in all likelihood, prefer his destruction to his assimilation. He was lacking the tools to articulate what his problem was and why he felt this way. He'd let his mind coast lazily for too long, and now he had nothing to fall back on aside from the very principles that Reece had debunked previously. He could not bring himself to reach the level of enlightenment that Reece had attained. Functionally, Oliver was no longer capable of lying to himself.

They turned a street corner passed an old eyeglasses repair shop and walked into an alleyway. It was the kind of alleyway you'd expect to be a permanent crime scene. Even with the dusk light still in the air it was pitch black in there. Edward led him to a metal spiral staircase that led to the upper level. At the front of the building the second floor looked like nothing but old bricks and dark windows. Oliver had never conceived that anything would exist within those walls and behind those windows.

Edward looked side to side with very shifty eyes, shiftier than Oliver had ever seen them. He scanned both entrances to the alleyway, made sure nobody was around, and then knocked a very complex pattern on the door.

"What's with the knock?" Oliver asked.

"If this place gets too well-known it'll get too crowded." Edward replied.

Whoever was behind the thick gray door began unlocking locks and unhooking hooks and eventually the door opened.

The room was lit with lanterns because nobody could get their hands on a dimmer switch anymore. The lanterns hung from the ceiling and blanketed the entire place with a gentle softness. Light that comes from a flame forces the edges of surfaces to blend together and creates a vague feeling of comfort, whereas the light that came out of that dreadful ceiling in the prison was harsh and hard. It made every shadow definite and exact. You could measure the shadows of hard light with a ruler, and that made them less compelling and relaxing. There were only five people in here and all of them had taken off their Insurrection uniforms because the heat from all of the lanterns would easily make you sweat right through the jacket. There was no bar, only a beat up pool table being used as a makeshift bar. The liquor was kept in an old white rickety bookcase that stood up against the wall behind the bartender. The man was oddly tiny for a bartender.

Oliver wondered how he could possibly keep rowdy patrons under control, but it was then he looked back towards the entrance to the bar as the door closed and there stood a massive man who looked like he could snap a man in half and think nothing of it. Behind the bar there was also a TV mounted to the wall above the bookcase. Delightful piano music was coming out of its tiny speakers, but the screen was off. A flash of relief filled Oliver when he discovered he'd be able to enjoy music without having to have the face of Reece in his peripheral.

The people in this place were mostly old folks. Three old women and two old men. Barstools were placed around the pool table on three sides. Oliver and Edward walked over to the bar. Edward took off his jacket, put it on the seat, and then sat on it. Oliver mimicked him.

"Who's this guy?" The bartender asked with a hint of mistrust.

"His name's Oliver. Good friend of mine. Don't worry, he won't tell anyone about this place."

"Better not. Too many people know about this place we'll get shut down. Only I get to give permission to people whether they can invite friends to come in. You can stay, just mind that fact."

Oliver was a bit nervous, but spoke formally to mask it, "Understood."

The bartender's face morphed from stern to welcoming quite quickly, "Good, now what'll you have?"

"You have beer?"

"Yep, one second."

The bartender walked into a separate room and then produced a small dark brown bottle. He placed it on the pool table without a coaster. The green felt was already covered in circular stains so there was no harm in it.

"Put it on my tab, Roger." Edward said.

"Got it," said Roger.

Oliver took a deep gulp of his beer. It tasted almost metallic, but he didn't care.

He turned to Edward, "How did you find this place? I'm surprised that you enjoy a place like this."

"Well, you were gone and I didn't have anyone," Edward started speaking a bit quieter and leaned into Oliver's ear, "Harry over there is selling his house and he wanted me to take some photos he could show to people. He didn't have enough money to pay me my standard rate so he brought me here instead and bought me a couple rounds. Trust me, the real payment was in showing me this place existed. I wouldn't have made it through all that stress without it. The people here are really nice. There are only like fifty of us that know about it. Tonight is when a few people come in to dance."

A few hours and more than a few rounds later Edward had been proven right. A group of about ten younger couples all arrived at the same time and Roger turned the speakers up on the television. They left all of their jackets near the entrance and began twirling and holding each other. As the people danced and more beer sloshed into Oliver's stomach he began to have prewar thoughts. He was completely released from the politics of it all for a while and he didn't even want to spite Reece anymore. It didn't matter to him what happened in Circle Park at this moment. All that mattered was that there were young couples in love in front of him, music playing, and booze melting his brain just enough to forget what he'd done for a short while.

One couple looked like they were getting tired and began slow dancing to every song, even if the song had a quick rhythm. He saw the woman leaning her chin up against the man's shoulder. Everything about her was captivating. She looked up at the man dancing with her, smiled, closed her eyes, and then dropped her chin back into his shoulder as they swayed back and forth to the tune. Her delicate hands rested on the man's shoulders as he dropped his chin and leaned further down, hoping to hold her slightly closer. She giggled and exposed a perfect array of shiny white teeth. She whispered something to her man and then she slumped completely into his arms playfully as if to say "please hold me I'm too exhausted to stand," the bottoms of her shoes were off of the ground as he supported the weight of her tiring body. She wasn't drunk whatsoever, just tired and in love. Her hair was long and wavy. Oliver was struck by her, and there was nothing impure about his desires either. Her ability to be both playful and elegant tugged at him.

But she was spoken for, and he knew that this was nothing more than some passing infatuation. Plus he would have to lie about most of his life for her to even be half-interested in someone like him. Although, the way things are, maybe his actions in the war would be something she'd approve of. For a brief moment he'd forgotten where he was. Time froze in place and everything was as it should be. He was drinking with a good friend, people were dancing and enjoying themselves, laughter and melodies echoed off the walls as the curves of the women's hips and the round shoulders of the men were accentuated by the flickering of the lanterns as they twirled one another around. All of their faces were soft and friendly, seemingly bereft of any political motivation whatsoever in the small secret pocket of light and warmth that had been kindled in this place. Perhaps unknowingly tending to the sides of themselves that were still human. He relished the feeling and even more pre-war thoughts began rushing in.

He remembered complaining to his mother about eating spaghetti and canned red sauce for the third night in a row. It was always a mystery why his parents enjoyed that meal so much until he was a teenager. It was not a voluntary choice, but a cheap and practical one. He remembers the horrific stench of the trash cans he had to eat out of during his trek into Insurrection territory. He remembers inventing a version of kickball as a kid where the kicker would sit on a swing, and the pitcher would time his throw as the kicker swung forward and it would launch the ball a superhuman distance.

Oliver tilted the nearly empty beer bottle toward his face and looked through it. The last swig sat at the bottom of the bottle and resembled a disgusting pale-yellow tongue awaiting a kiss. He drank the last bit of beer and stumbled toward the bathroom in a stupor.

The walls in here were cracked, the mirror was smashed, and there were no dividing walls between toilets. Oliver did his business, proceeded to wash his hands, and clumsily held himself up by only rinsing one hand at a time and making sure the other hand was stabilizing his intoxicated body. He made sure to keep staring at his hand in the sink because looking at himself in the broken shards of glass was out of the question. As he was finishing up Edward burst through the bathroom door.

"Everyone is heading out Reece is giving a speech. At night! I've never seen a nighttime speech before it must be important! Hurry up let's go! The bouncer's going to leave soon and he *will* lock you in here!" Edward said frantically as he rushed back into the main room.

Too drunk to answer him and barely able to stand, Oliver tried to compose himself. By the time he steadied his body enough to exit the bathroom he saw the bouncer's back as he shut the door to the bar. The lanterns were all snuffed out and the tinted windows barely let any of the moonlight in. The room was silent. The music was gone. The laughter had stopped. The warmth was slowly dissipating and Oliver was again forced to remember where he actually was. Everyone, even Edward, had abandoned him. Left him to rot in the dark. Oliver's eyes adjusted to the darkness and he walked toward the door to the bar. There was one lock that required a key to unlock from the inside. He then gracelessly shuffled behind the pool table and found a nearly empty bottle of bourbon sitting at the bottom of the bookshelf.

He sat up against the wall and finished the last few gulps left in the bottle, and then he collapsed onto the floor, with thoughts in his head about what he and that woman's children might've looked like if only he had made a few better choices, and if only he hadn't treated love, for so long, like a menacing distraction from what was truly important in life.

CHAPTER FOURTEEN

Something hard hit him in the ribs. Oliver let out a strained yelp. He opened his eyes and saw a grimy brown shoe, he moved his eyes upward along a pair of large wrinkly jeans and saw the stern face of the bouncer. The man had a fat neck and head, but the rest of his body wasn't nearly as squishy.

"Come on, up. Get up!" He said in a low growl.

"I am. I am." Oliver said as he tried to force himself upright. His stomach was screaming and his head was pounding. The tastes of bile and metal filled his mouth. During the course of the night he woke up at least three times and rushed to the bathroom to puke. At least that's what must've happened because the floor in front of him was still spotless aside from the empty bottle of bourbon. He had blurry memories from last night. All he could remember definitively was what the woman from last night looked like, and the fact that Edward had completely abandoned him to be locked in a bar overnight so that he wouldn't miss Reece's speech.

As he struggled to muster up the will to stand, the bouncer forced him up by grabbing the inside of his elbow and dragging him to his feet.

"We're getting ready for tonight. Get out."

"I'm going. I'm going." Oliver replied.

"Damn right you are."

Oliver was pulled to the door by the bouncer, stumbling over himself with every step and then was thrown onto the small second story platform, nearly falling down the spiral metal staircase and landing on his side.

"We open in an hour. Roger has a three strike rule. Tomorrow you're limited to two drinks. Don't let it happen again." The bouncer roared as he slammed the door. Oliver pulled himself to his feet again just long enough to reach the dingy alleyway, then he collapsed again and leaned his back up against the cold concrete wall of the opposite building. Trash bags that had accumulated from the night before surrounded him, as did various stains of piss and discarded cigarette butts.

No child hopes to end up like this. No young lad arises from a deep sleep and tells their parents of the wondrous dream they had of having a throbbing headache, being on the verge of vomiting, and stinking of garbage. Every muscle of his was sore from supporting the weight of every person he did not love, every life he did not live, every dish he had never tasted, every friend he did not make, every small act of kindness he refused to undertake, every book he'd never read, every thought he'd never had, and every happy memory he never made.

He looked to his left and caught a glimpse of two middle-aged women walking down the street with cups of coffee. There was no way to make out what they were saying, but it reminded him of what life used to be like, at least what he imagined life used to be like before everyone had to filter their every action and every perceived reality through this accursed Philosophy. How did one end up justifying the act of buying a cup of hot coffee and casually walking down the street with it?

It gave the drinker energy and one couldn't possibly assist the Insurrection in its goals if they were lacking energy, and in addition to that it was a boost to the internal economy of the Insurrection? Oliver wished he could just say that he wanted a hot coffee because he was cold, and the drink was warm, and feeling a warm beverage seep into your stomach and coat your insides with relaxation was a beautiful feeling. To just dance, to light a match for nothing but the smell of smoking sulfur, doing things because of themselves. But alas, that was too romantic a view of things and the only "rational" process of thought was strategic.

People no longer refrained from immoral behavior because it was "the wrong thing to do," but solely so that the enemy could not accuse them of it. "Don't give them ammo," was a phrase used on the regular before the war. Everything was done to serve the furtherance of an argument and people lived their lives as if they weren't human, and instead, existed as mere premises in a very important abstract political syllogism. To stray from the strict behavioral requirements of a worthwhile premise, was to alter or disprove the conclusion, and the conclusion was what one based their political opinion on in the first place.

They would bleed themselves dry financially, abandon their relationships, isolate themselves from the world, and behave in all sorts of unconscionable ways for the sole purpose of being a dutiful premise that the enemy could not take advantage of while standing at the podium, and the sick ironic reason for this base destruction of everyone's inner humanity was a "desire for consistency." If someone's arguments ran counter to what they truly desired in life, to a fundamental part of their identity, to a harmless activity they enjoyed, or a loving relationship with someone else that they had, the argument won out, and the human decided they must fashion themselves around the argument instead of taking dictation from the quiet honest sighs of their true selves. Eventually the true self atrophies, then disintegrates, and the cognitive dissonance that comes with intentionally propagandizing is lost. Your identity becomes completely subsumed. If you can get an entire population to this stage of enlightenment, then you can steer them anywhere, and not a single one of them will have a care in the world which direction they're going in.

An eye for an eye levels the playing field.

He cycled this thought through his head over and over again, trying to find a correct objection. What was it that was so naturally off-putting about this formulation? If the enemy takes your eye, and you're in some competition where sight is required, then taking their eye is reasonable if your goal is to win. Why hinder oneself? This bounced around Oliver's skull, along with the corpse of Alex, the wails of the injured man he stepped on, Edward's worried face, Reece's manic stares, and the static of his television. Why did he hate himself for killing Alex if the Vigil would've done the very same thing? Why did the Philosophy of Advantage not guard him against this feeling anymore? Nothing. He could come up with nothing, and the hate remained. There was no context outside of the war any longer, but he yearned for that context to be carved out somewhere. This bar was all he had now. A piss-poor refuge from his cowardice, ineffectiveness, and insignificance.

Early evening gave way to dusk which in turn gave way to night. Oliver sat there in the dingy alleyway for a couple of hours watching the occasional person file in and deliver the secret knock. He was in such a miserable state, hungry and hung over, and it was unlikely the bouncer would let him in again after causing him so much trouble that afternoon. He didn't dare go home either for fear of what he might say to Edward in a rage if he ran into him. So there he sat, comfortable with the idea that he would sleep among garbage until the next day. His chest began to feel both light and heavy simultaneously, his heart began racing, his upper cheeks tingled slightly, and his mouth contorted to a despairing wide half-smile. Nobody frowns naturally when they cry. Sobbing always sounds suspiciously like someone with a clogged nose trying to laugh.

"Oliver," said Edward as he strolled through the alleyway.

"Hey," Oliver said.

"Why didn't you come home?" Edward asked.

"No reason just...a lot." Oliver replied.

"A lot? What do you mean a lot? You're sitting in trash. Here get up." Edward extended his hand and Oliver refused it.

"I'll get up myself," Oliver said, averting his eyes.

"Okay...maybe you should go home."

"No, I'm going in with you. I have some things to say to you."

"Alright, are you upset?"

"Edward, I'm livid."

"Why?"

"Inside."

They walked up the staircase once again and Edward executed a perfect rendition of the bar's secret knock. As they entered, the bouncer glared at Oliver until he sat down at the pool table and made it clear that he was only reluctantly welcome. It was incredible how quickly he already frivolously stomped on thin ice in what seemed to be the only haven that existed away from the violence and polemics beyond the front door.

Oliver decided to stray away from beer and order hard liquor. He'd banked on the bartender having a generous pour because there was no way two bottles of beer would get him comfortably drunk enough to confront the only true friend he's ever had. They both sat down at the pool table. Edward refused to make eye contact with Oliver and kept his gaze pointed towards the table, the other patrons, and the ceiling, much like a child who knew he was in for a very aggressive lecture from a disappointed parent.

"What'll it be?" Roger asked, "Ed, you're aware your friend here only gets two?"

"Yes," Edward said, "I'll take vodka."

Roger looked back toward a slouching Oliver, "And you?"

"Look, I want to apologize for my conduct last night. I've just been..."

"Agh, don't worry about it," Roger replied, "Trust me, I know what it's like to not drink for a long time and then fall off the wagon. No need to explain yourself to me."

"Thanks. I'll take Rye if you have it."

"Only got one kinda Rye, and it's fifty two percent. Guessing that's fine?"

"Yeah," Oliver said.

Oliver turned towards Edward and saw that he was facing away from him. This was too much to put on the poor man. His friend paid for his drinks, never lost hope in his return while he was in prison, threatened to burn the pamphlet while the Protocol was being issued so he'd stay safe, and had kept the secret of his changed allegiance despite the looming consequences. Edward was a good man, but they would never be able to connect as equals again.

"Ed, we don't have to have the fight." Oliver said.

"I thought about reporting you, you know?" Edward said quietly and angrily as he turned around in his seat.

"What?"

"That's right. I thought you'd lost it. That you went insane."

"I haven't, Ed."

"Ever since you got back you've been drunk. Every goddamned night. Do you realize what that's done to me?"

"There are reasons for this."

Edward's voice got louder and he leaned forward.

"Are they good ones? All the time you're either hammered or asking stupid questions. I'm sorry that I'm getting so mad, but you make life so fucking difficult. I've got *your* doubts swimming around in my head and I can't talk to anyone else about them! Do you understand how maddening that is? I don't know the answers to all of your questions, and I don't know how to stop you from being miserable. The least you could do is show me a little respect and not piss all over yourself and tarnish my reputation in this place."

"Ed, please..."

"It's not *my* fault that you can't justify to yourself why I would still support the Insurrection. You think I'm an idiot don't you?"

"Ed!" Oliver shouted, "Enough. I get it."

The bouncer began to take a few steps away from the door.

Edward slinked back down in his seat, "I'm done being afraid of you and worried about you, Oliver. I'm not paying for your drink either."

"It's fine," Oliver said as the bartender put their drinks down on the table.

"The second I leave to get your drinks you two are fighting. What the hell are you fighting about?"

"Nothing," Edward said as he shot Oliver a paranoid glance, "It's nothing."

"No it's not nothing," Roger said. "I'm going to call the bouncer over to chuck you both out if you don't tell me. We're going to resolve this right now. Markus, come here please." Roger said. The bouncer took a few more steps toward the picnic table until he was standing directly behind them.

Oliver spoke up, "He was angry with me for getting drunk last night and sleeping in the bar. Thought I ruined his reputation here. That's it."

"No, I heard comments about the Insurrection and propaganda. I don't want any Vigil bullshit in this bar. Tell me what you two were actually arguing about. Ed, what's the deal?"

Nowhere was safe. Oliver's eyes drooped and his adrenaline left his body. There was no Victory available to him. He wasn't welcome anywhere. He turned his head to look at Edward with apologetic eyes. Edward shook his head side to side nearly imperceptibly, but it was too late. Oliver had made his choice. What should've been done from the start.

"During the Protocol I went on a mission with Reece and he made me murder a Vigil child."

Roger looked confused, "Alright, and?"

Oliver looked towards the ceiling at the flickering lanterns. Tears began to well up in his eyes. The sheer carelessness of it. The blatant sociopathy. That "and" hung in the air with a putrid lingering stink. Edward stood up and began to back away from the pool table as Oliver said, "Alright and? Alright fucking and? I no longer support Victory over the Vigil."

Markus boomed, "What the fuck did you just say?" as he grabbed Oliver by the back of the collar.

He dragged him into the alleyway, and threw him down on the concrete. Oliver's face twisted into a relieved but quivering smile. Markus descended the stairs, lifted his foot and slammed his heel against Oliver's rib cage. The sounds of his bones cracking were muffled by exhausted screeches of pain. Markus' fist connected with Oliver's nose as he tried to sit up, forcing the back of his head to smash against the ground and blood to start leaking out of his face. A few more blows to the head caused his lips to swell as his teeth mashed into the back of his mouth.

Just finish it already

Oliver didn't bother to try and get up as Markus left to grab an aluminum bat that was hidden in a corner of the bar. Roger and a few patrons filed outside to join, giving Oliver's stomach and face a good beating. It was possible that raising his arms in the air and shouting out that he also doesn't support the Vigil achieving Victory over the Insurrection might prevent them from killing him, but at that moment, the side of Oliver that wanted to die held the power. They would've thought he was lying and just trying to avoid the beating. Of course, once one indicates that they don't support the Insurrection, a switch flips in the brain of every member. Pre-confession, he could be trusted and so his statement of dissent is treated as the raw truth, but post-confession he was now considered a liar, an evil man, someone who could never be trusted.

"Fuckin' kill the bastard!" One of them shouted from the second story.

Edward just stood there. Frozen in panic.

"I'm sorry, Oliver. I'm so sorry," Edward whispered.

Roger and the other patrons backed off as Markus returned wielding the rather small blue-tinted metal bat. Markus struck him once across the face, but there was no pain. Oliver wasn't given enough time to let the violence age from trauma to radiating agony. All he felt was the burning and aching sensation in his ribs. All it gave him time for were thoughts. Little pieces of thought between the beatings. Markus reared the bat back a second time and struck Oliver squarely in the forehead. The bat dented his skull ever so slightly.

I'm sorry Ed

The second blow came down in exactly the same spot causing his skull to crack.

Bright blue sky. Green grass. No more dreaming.

The third blow caused fragments of his skull to pierce into his brain and it ended him for good, but Markus did not let up. He beat Oliver's face until it was unrecognizable and left him there in the alley, with Roger and the patrons laughing as they retreated back into the bar, but not before banning Edward from ever returning.

The moment his world retreated into nothingness,

he had achieved precisely what he needed to achieve in order to forgive himself for killing that boy. Oliver forced them to kill him over something they never would've believed was a crime in the first place. The crime, to them, was not the murder, but something else entirely. As tends to happen, the birds had come home. The executioner hewn in two with a bloody axe, the feet of the hangman twirled slowly in the air, and the wannabe martyr stabbed through the heart with a wooden cross that he'd sharpened himself.

Edward stood there for a few moments frozen, but when the shock of what he witnessed wore off he doubled over and began weeping and gagging. His heart in total anguish over his friend's murder, but his stomach unable to cope with a dead body or the stress. He couldn't initially accept the transition between "Oliver" and "Oliver's body." No longer able to stop himself, Edward cursed the Insurrection, cursed the men inside of the bar, and cursed both Reece and Nicholas. Despite his vocal chords twitching with desperate angst to shout these denunciations into every tranquil crevice that had enjoyed serine silence for years, he could only clench his fists, grit his teeth, and allow his brain to pulse and flex with these statements of fury.

He'd scoffed at the complex and impersonal paperwork smattered world before the war and yearned for a world bombed back into simplicity, where everything was easily understandable, where good and evil wore obvious uniforms, where the color gray had its throat slashed and its corpse buried in soft black dirt under the watchful eye of a bright white sky, and where they could comfortably shut their minds off and receive their orders from orthodox sociopaths. Edward thought this would lead to an honest world, in a twisted way, where everyone was up front about their hatreds, admirations, and somehow, their dishonesty. Instead, it led him here. His knees being pierced by tiny flecks of gravel, trying to conceal his heathenish sobbing while his best friend's blood slowly froze against a piss-stained concrete wall.

CHAPTER FIFTEEN

It was raining heavily as Reece took the podium on the steps of the old state house overlooking Circle Park. The droplets sounded like thousands of little firing pins sounding off in the middle of a brutal firefight. The corpses of the leaves were being carried by a weak current flowing along the sidewalk. On occasion there would be an incline in the concrete and the leaves, riddled with wounds, would bunch up into a grotesque pile and form a miniature whirlpool where the broken stems and torn husks of the plants swirled around one another as the raindrops crashed into their exposed bellies from above.

The gutters of the triple decker buildings were flushing the accumulated muck into the street, and people with bright Insurrection torches seared onto their jackets began to gather in the grass. Rusty construction machines were bunched around the tree that stood in the center of Circle Park, their gigantic metal teeth chomping through the damp Earth with marvelous speed. The engines roared and the hinges creaked with each shovel full of wet muck and made sure to avoid damaging the memorial headstones of the Circle Park Ten.

Edward's camera hung from his neck and was hidden under his uniform jacket to protect it from the rain. As the crowd grew in size, he retreated under the awning of a closed thrift shop and lit a cigarette. The smoke singed the insides of his lungs with his first inhale, forcing an initial gasp and a couple of weak coughs.

This was the first time he'd picked up a pack in years, but he wasn't allowed in the bar anymore, and he needed something to deal with the constant stress. He sat down on the small staircase that led to the shop's entrance and prepared his camera for the upcoming spectacle. Quickly, he snapped photos of the machinery and took a few candid shots of people jogging down the street in excitement. Shoving the photos into his jacket pocket, he disposed of the cigarette and began walking into the park.

Reece stood there perfectly still aside from his head slowly swiveling from side to side scanning every individual person who made their way into the crowd. His hands were clasped behind his back and his face was near expressionless aside from the occasional twitching of the brow and pursing of the lips. The operators of the excavation equipment had finished their job. They exited the vehicles, walked up to Reece, and whispered something into his ear.

A couple of audience members slowly moved toward the holes in the ground and looked into them, and looks of visible confusion appeared on their faces. They began rapidly looking at one another and pointing to the bottom of the holes. Edward needed to see what was going on, it might be necessary for the next Weekly Report. Clearly this is was a big deal. He pulled his coat collar upwards, hunched over to try and prevent rain from leaking onto the camera, and began marching forward toward the unearthed graves. As he approached, more people began surrounding the area.

Edward needed to push past a few bystanders to get a decent shot of whatever was inside the graves. Leaning over the edge of the wet and slowly collapsing pits, he saw nothing. There was nothing. No remains, no coffin. It was completely devoid of former life. Edward began rushing to the other graves and this fact was consistent among all of them. He nervously fished the camera from out of his jacket and began taking pictures. One of the grave stones and one of an empty grave. He anxiously shoved them into his pockets.

How was this possible?

"Please, ladies and gentlemen, step away from the graves. You've all seen it by now. I need to speak on this subject," Reece boomed into his microphone.

The audience trickled away from the machinery and congealed right in front of the podium, they were all eager for an explanation, for a resolution to this contradiction, for a justifiable reason for this apparent decades long campaign of false propaganda, not just enacted against the Vigil, but enacted against them.

"Brothers and sisters of the Insurrection and loyal adherents to the Philosophy of Advantage, it has been brought to my attention that there have been doubts circulating about the nature of the Circle Park Ten and what happened on that fateful day. As can easily be shown by the lack of human remains inside of the graves, it's quite obvious that the alleged first warriors and casualties in our great struggle do not rest where we have originally presumed. This is just as big a shock to me as it is to you. Of course, our first course of action should be to resolve this contradiction between what we are seeing and what our argument against the Vigil hinges on."

Edward snapped a few pictures of Reece delivering his speech and stored them. The crowd was eerily silent. Men, women, and children alike were eagerly awaiting each individual word.

"How does our Philosophy dictate we must handle this, ladies and gentlemen, how can we possibly recover from this intellectual blow?"

Reece then looked behind him and gestured for someone to come out of the statehouse. Ten men began filing out, each of them carrying a dead body and a uniform jacket.

"I would be a terrible leader if I did not have a contingency plan for something like this, and it would prove my Philosophy to be quite weak if it were unable to stand up to this kind of challenge, but ladies and gentlemen, I've come up with a way to resolve this contradiction and maintain the Insurrection's intellectual high-ground."

Edward took a photo of the ten men lined up with the bodies in their arms.

"These dead men are either executed Vigil prisoners or would-be defectors from the Insurrection."

Reece then motioned the men towards the excavated graves. The ten stone-faced men waddled passed the vehicles and placed each of the bodies near the edge of each hole. They then lifted the torsos of each body so that they were leaning forward in a sitting position, and placed the spare Insurrection jacket, imbued with the red torch, on their backs, gently guiding an arm through each sleeve, then rolled them into the uncomfortably vacant pockets of Earth. Then the construction workers got up to the tasks of burying the bodies.

"As per the Philosophy, ladies and gentlemen, our contradiction is now resolved. When asked about whether there are Insurrection bodies buried in those graves, we are now able to answer in the affirmative. When Vigil propaganda whimpers and moans with incessant stupidity and ignorance that we are lying about what occurred in Circle Park that day, we are able to answer with confidence that they are incorrect in their assessment. For if anyone tries to unearth these graves again, in future generations, it will be shown that we were correct about the major question of the age. These bodies will decay, and all that will remain will be the torch of the Insurrection, burning brightly for all coming time."

The crowd roared with excitement.

"Genius, absolute genius," one of the crowd members exclaimed.

Edward was getting worried as the fervor of the crowd grew and grew in admiration of Reece's shrewd political cunning. His stomach twisted and he had to retreat out of the crowd to process what had just happened. Oliver was wrong in his assessment. No exposure of truth, no recognition of reality, not even a convincing rhetorical case could be crafted against Reece's Philosophy of Advantage. Not even a complete negation of the war's cause was compelling enough to render him, or his political standing, weaker. The people were perfectly willing to accept that they had been lied to, provided that they got to join in on the lie. They loved the lie. It was a convincing lie. They thought the lie cunning. They thought the lie righteous.

They thought the lie important strategically and philo-sophically. The truth of the last few decades of human thought, death, war, famine, strife, fear, cruelty, and insanity had been revealed for the wandering eye to behold, and none of it mattered. It had been massaged into the brain of every living person that the truth was a liability, and as such, was ineffective in fighting anything. Reality had been rendered as useless as a blunt sword. A discarded instrument of a bygone era. There was no "point" to the settling of factual disputes whatsoever. The Philosophy's venomous barbs laced across its tendrils had wrapped everyone in a predatory embrace and ripped its way through their organs. They had finally freed themselves, completely, from all of those tired old conceptions, all of those cute childish illusions that once oppressed the political mind.

There was no higher cause for this struggle. There were no pretenses of justice, no reference to objectivity, and no moral high ground upon which to fight. There existed no case for survival any longer. They were not fighting *for* anything but raw power which, in turn, translated to political success. No greater good was made weighty in their hearts, and there was no actual political platform articulated. People knew they were fighting over nothing, knew that they had mobilized over something completely fictional, knew as an undis-puted fact that they were destroying each other for no good reason at all, and they *liked* it.

Storing the last of his photos, Edward lit another cigarette and rushed home. He grabbed his keys with shaking hands, unlocked his door, and stumbled inside. His flop sweat mixed with the rain water covering his forehead, and a few droplets irritated his eyes. He took a few moments to catch his breath and undress. Edward threw his jacket to the floor and was breathing uncomfortably heavily. He opened the pack of cigarettes again and lit another one as he fished the photographs from out of his jacket pocket. Tossing them onto his desk and spreading them out, he examined each and every one of them. The empty hole, the limp bodies, the machinery, and Reece standing there in all his smug overbearing glory.

Oliver had walked a dangerous line, but at least he had a brief window to experience some sort of individual fulfillment. Edward finally understood why, in his final moments, his friend could not stop smiling and bearing his bloodied teeth. All they could do was kill him.

Edward lifted the photo of the empty grave off of the desk and stared at it for a few moments. The choice was his. Surrounding him was a vast pitch black tunnel. Behind him were iron bars, and through the bars there was a dull flickering torch. One could never reach that light, take it for themselves, but it illuminated the immediate area and gave off just enough warmth for survival. In front of him was a colossal span of dark nothingness in all directions, but in the distance, there was what looked like a microscopic shimmer. A glow that tempted the soul to take the risk, abandon the weak smoldering flame they've become so used to and reach for the unknown.

Edward opened the top drawer on the right side of his desk and looked inside. Last week's "Weekly Report" rested there with all of his photo submissions. He opened the top drawer to the left and his friend's blank "Oliver Column" sat there, accumulating dust and resentment. Edward fell back into his chair and pressed his palms to his forehead. Ruminating about every possible consequence and whether this was worth the trouble. Just then there was a knock at his door.

He slammed the drawers shut and called out, "Business is closed for the day!"

"Not here for business," the man on the other side said.

Edward began panicking, "Well, who is it then?"

"Harry, you took a bunch of pictures for my house, heard the story about your friend."

"Alright, alright come in." Edward said.

He unlocked his door and Harry strolled in.

"Please, have a seat." Edward said as he gestured to the loveseat in the corner of the room.

"Just wanted to come by and give you my condolences," Harry said.

"That's awfully kind of you, but unnecessary. He was my friend for a long time around here and we did pretty much everything together. I'm still trying to figure out how to grieve over this." Edward said.

"Yeah, can't imagine I'd be grieving if I found out my friend was a Vigil agent this whole time. Shame they'd go after the nice people too, I guess they're quicker to trust." Harry said.

Edward gripped the arm of his chair tighter and tried to force his mouth to stay closed. How dare this man who barely knew Oliver try to smear him like this? He was nowhere close to becoming a Vigil agent for his entire life.

That was just the nature of the two collective minds which existed in the country. If you were not the one, you were, by definition, the other. Yet, if you weren't the other, you were, by definition, the one, and in order to keep this claustrophobic way of being alive the one and the other must forever touch.

"Y...yeah," Edward said as he stared with sad rage into Harry's eyes.

"I didn't mean to upset you, maybe it was a mistake coming here," Harry said.

"Maybe," Edward responded as he shifted in his seat.

"I'll get out of your hair then. I'm sorry if I offended you, Ed." Harry said.

"Edward."

"Huh?"

"My name is Edward," Edward said.

"Okay, clearly I've crossed some sort of line. I'm going to leave, but I wanted to ask when you'd be open again."

"Please just get out, Harry. Just get out." Edward said softly, but sternly.

"Sorry," Harry said as he shut the door behind him.

Edward locked his front door and returned to his photographs. He gathered them into a pile, tapped them on the desk, and put them in the drawer with the "Weekly Report." The radiance of the distant light beckoned to him just as it had called to Oliver. Edward had finally understood him, and the transfer of doubt was complete. He snatched the photo of the empty grave, gently placed it inside the opposite drawer over his friend's blank column, locked it, and stared with passive misery at the dim, cold, and quivering shadows of his feet. He bleakly accepted this fate, and allowed his humanity to be ground to dust between two enormous blocks of bone and teeth, which had agreed a long time ago to slowly shave pieces off of one another for as long as they could possibly manage.

ACKNOWLEDGMENTS

I would like to thank all of the various giants that have allowed me a brief moment of time to view the world from their shoulders, and those who graciously dealt with me throughout this process of writing this book.

ABOUT THE AUTHOR

Justin Little is a journalist, essayist and novelist based out of Boston. He is the author of *The Misadventures of a Jilted Journalist*. This is his second book.

Follow him on Twitter @Vernaculis

www.ingramcontent.com/pod-product-compliance
Lightning Source LLC
Chambersburg PA
CBHW050409190726
48284CB00007BB/2497